For The Keeper's Chronicles

"No one tickles the funnybone and chills the blood better than Tanya Huff , who does both exceedingly well in her wonderful new novel….With screamingly funny dialogue and sharp plotting, Ms. Huff makes every word a positively delightful experience in this imaginative tale."

—Romantic Time

"Fans of humorous fantasy will enjoy this fast-moving tale, as will cat lovers and anyone else who can suspend their disbelief and settle back for a good time."

—Voya

For the Valor Series

"The notable Tanya Huff proves herself equally adept at military as contemporary fantasy in her riveting *Valor's Choice*… Ms. Huff captures the ambiance of an elite military group and adds a rare depth to skillful characterization to make each personality stand up and be counted."

—Romantic Times

"An intriguing alien race, a likeable protagonist, a fast moving plot, and a rousing ending. What more could you ask for?"

—Science Fiction Chronicle

For *The Silvered*

"Tanya Huff is a long-time favorite read of mine, and *The Silvered* is an amazing book… Unexpected twists and turns abound. I loved this book."

—Charlaine Harris, #1 New York Times bestselling author

ALSO BY TANYA HUFF

The Victory Nelson "Blood" Series
Blood Price
Blood Trail
Blood Lines
Blood Pact
Blood Debt
Blood Bank *

The Tony "Smoke" Series
Smoke and Shadows
Smoke and Mirrors
Smoke and Ashes

The Torin Kerr Series
VALOR NOVELS
Valor's Choice ‡
The Better Part of Valor ‡
The Heart of Valor
Valor's Trial
The Truth of Valor

PEACEKEEPER NOVELS
An Ancient Peace

The Quarters Series
Sing the Four Quarters †
Fifth Quarter †
No Quarter †
The Quartered Sea †

The Keeper's Chronicles
Summon the Keeper
The Second Summoning
Long Hot Summoning

The Enchantment Emporium Series
The Enchantment Emporium
The Wild Ways
The Future Falls

Wizard of the Grove
Child of the Grove
Wizard of the Grove

Standalone Novels
The Fire's Stone
Gate of Darkness, Circle of Light
The Silvered

Short Story Collections
What Ho, Magic!
Stealing Magic
Relatively Magic
Finding Magic
Nights of the Round Table †
February Thaw †
Third Time Lucky †
He Said, Sidhe Said †
Swan's Braid & Other Tales of Terizan †

* *a short story collection*
† *available as a Jabberwocky ebook*
‡ *also available in the omnibus*
A Confederation of Valor

Praise for Tanya Huff's Novels

For the Quarters Series

"Huff has created a romantic fantasy that offers the reader a sometimes feisty but always intelligent, vocal and vigorous heroine."

—Voya

"Only a storyteller of Ms. Huff's considerable merit could create the extraordinary characterization to bring this unusual storyline to full and vivid life."

—Romantic Times

"A favorite book means to me one you reread frequently and know you will enjoy even with flu. Out of a shelf-full of such, the one my hand goes to most unerringly is Tanya Huff's *Sing The Four Quarters*. I love this book for being both very funny and wholly serious about the elemental spirits and about justice, mercy, love, kindness and honor."

—Diana Wynne Jones,
on her selection for her favorite fantasy novel
for The Washington Post Book World

For the Enchantment Emporium Series

"Tanya Huff crams so much delightful stuff into her books that they deserve to be slowly unpacked…The story emerges from a dazzling array of character and detail… The magic is deftly handled, the family stuff is bewildering and gripping, and the humour is as sharp as a dragon's tooth."

—Daily Mail

"A delight from start to finish — by turns humorous, romantic and dramatic. So far, this is easily one of my favorite books of the year."
— Charles de Lint for Fantasy and Science Fiction

For the Blood Series

"Readers will stay on the edge of their seats… smashing entertainment for a wide audience."

—Romantic Times

"*Blood Price* still stands up as an urban fantasy, and a darn good one too. So, if you enjoy mysteries and fantasy with a bite, check it out."

—SF Revue

For the Smoke Series

"It's a wild romp, full of dark humor, a delightfully twisted version of the usual haunted house story."

—Locus

"Fans of Buffy and The X-files will cheer the latest exploits of Tony Foster… This spinoff from Huff's popular Blood series stands alone as an entertaining supernatural adventure…"

—Publishers Weekly

For *The Fire's Stone*

"The delightful camaraderie of three unlikely heroes and well-controlled fantasy elements that are integral to the plot make Huff's adventure great fun to read."

—Publishers Weekly

For *Gate of Darkness, Circle of Light*

"Huff's real-world fantasy presents an enlightened, compassionate view of the forgotten heroes of urban society. High recommended."

—Library Journal

"Contemporary urban fantasy at its best."

—Locus

The Demon's Den

and Other Tales of Valdemar

In the World Created by Mercedes Lackey

TANYA HUFF

Published by JABberwocky Literary Agency, Inc.

The Demon's Den and Other Tales of Valdemar

Copyright © 2018 by Tanya Huff
All rights reserved.

The characters and events portrayed in this book are fictitious. Any similarity to real persons, living or dead, is coincidental and not intended by the author.

This paperback edition published in 2018 by
JABberwocky Literary Agency, Inc.

Publication History:

"The Demon's Den" originally published in *Sword of Ice and Other Tales of Valdemar*, DAW Books Inc., 1997 and collected in *Finding Magic*, ISFIC Press, 2007.

"Brock" originally published in *Sun in Glory and Other Tales of Valdemar*, DAW Books Inc., 2003 and collected in *Finding Magic*, ISFIC Press, 2007.

"All the Ages of Man" originally published in *Crossroads and Other Tales of Valdemar*, DAW Books Inc., 2005 and collected in *Finding Magic*, ISFIC Press, 2007.

"Live On" originally published in *Moving Targets and Other Tales of Valdemar*, DAW Books Inc., 2008.

"Nothing Better to Do" originally published in *Changing the World: All-New Tales of Valdemar*, DAW Books Inc., 2009.

"The Time We Have" originally published in *Finding the Way and Other Tales of Valdemar*, DAW Books Inc., 2010.

"Family Matters" originally published in *Under the Way and Other Tales of Valdemar*, DAW Books Inc., 2011.

Cover design by Tiger Bright Studios.

ISBN 978-1-625673-73-2

CONTENTS

INTRODUCTION

I want to thank Mercedes Lackey for generously allowing me to publish these stories set in her world. If you're reading, because you're a Tanya Huff reader and are unfamiliar with the Valdemar books, I hope you give them a try. If you're here because you're a Valdemar fan and wanted to read the Jors stories all in one place, thank you. I hope you give my other work a try.

Now, how did this come about?

Back in the mid 1980s, I sold *Child of the Grove* to DAW Books; un-agented. I had no idea of how to get an agent, but I knew I should have one, so as I did rewrites and waited for *Child* to come out and wrote an outline for my next book, I poked at the agent thing. Now, DAW had recently published Mercedes Lackey's *Arrows of the Queen* (1987 to *Child's*

1988), and I thought to myself, here's someone who's just a little ahead of me publishing-wise, maybe she knows about this whole agent thing.

I honestly don't remember how I got in contact with her. I suspect I asked someone at DAW to pass on my number. Point is, we talked. And Misty was very helpful. And then when I had copy edit questions, we talked again. Then we kept talking. Mostly email. Some letters. A few phone calls. I sent her my manuscripts; she sent me hers.

Back in the day, we printed our books on fanfold paper. For those of you too young to have ever worked with fanfold, manuscripts had to be separated a page at a time and the guide… um… edges had to be taken off before it was mailed it to the editor. When Misty and I mailed manuscripts to each other, we didn't bother. Generally, I separated pages as I read, or I unfolded on one side of me and refolded on the other. One day, Fiona came home from work to find our small apartment full of paper. Misty had sent me *Magic's Pawn* and I was so completely enthralled, I read the entire book as though it were printed on one long page, allowing the un-fanfolded paper to billow up around me.

Then I sent Misty my response. I'm paraphrasing, it was a long time ago, but the gist of it was, "You know the silence that comes after an amazing performance, before the applause?

This is yours."

So, I have some history with Valdemar.

Back in 1996, Misty told me about plans for an anthology

of Valdemar stories and asked if I'd write a story for it. I was honoured to be asked, but wow, what a responsibility. People loved the Valdemar books and it wasn't just the world building that needed to be right, but the feel. The Valdemar books are filled with hope, and joy, and characters learning to be better than they are. Could I do that?

Misty seemed to think so. She thought so seven times. (There've been more than seven anthologies, but I'd finished Jors' story at seven and stepped away.)

This is where you get to decide if you agree.

There been some discussion among writers about collecting earlier work. Do we fix errors? Polish a little? Or do we leave them intact, as is, as a historical record? I come down on the fix and polish side. The original stories are out there, in print, if you want to read them; the historical record secured. This e-collection is my chance to do a little tweaking and make them even better than they were. The stories haven't been changed, nor have the characters, but a few awkward clauses have been smoothed out, and a problem no one noticed the first time around has been corrected. Because I'm working from the submission manuscripts, not the published text, many commas have been moved. Or removed. Or both. You deserve the best. So does Valdemar.

January 2018

THE DEMON'S DEN

The mine had obviously been abandoned for years. Not even dusk hid the broken timbers and the scree of rock that spilled out of the gaping black hole.

Jors squinted into the wind, trying and failing to see past the shadows. *:Are you sure it went in there?:*

:Of course I'm sure. I can smell the blood trail.:

:Maybe it's not hurt as badly as we thought. Maybe it'll be fine until morning.: His Companion gave a little buck. Jors clutched at the saddle and sighed. *:All right, all right, I'm going.:*

No one at the farmstead had known why the mountain cat had come down out of the heights. Perhaps the deer it normally hunted had grown scarce. Perhaps a more aggressive cat had driven it from its territory. Perhaps it had grown lazy and decided sheep were less work. No one at the farmstead cared. They'd tried to drive it off. It had retaliated by mauling a shepherd and three dogs. Now, they wanted it killed.

Just my luck to be riding circuit up here in the great white north. Jors swung out of the saddle and pulled his gloves off with his teeth. *:How am I supposed to shoot it when I won't be able to see it?:* he asked, unstrapping his bow.

Gervis turned his head to peer back at his Chosen with one sapphire eye. *:It's hurt.:*

:I know.: The wind sucked the heat out of his hands, and he swore under his breath as one of the laces of his small pack knotted tight.

:You wounded it.:

:I know, damn it. I know!: Sighing, he rested his head on the Companion's warm flank. *:I'm sorry. It's just been a long day, and I should never have missed that shot.:*

:No one makes every shot, Chosen.:

The warm understanding in the mindspeech helped.

The cat had been easy to track. By late afternoon, they'd known they were close. At sunset, they spotted it outlined against a grey and glowering sky. Jors had carefully aimed, carefully let fly, and watched in horror as the arrow thudded deep into a golden haunch. The cat had screamed and fled. They'd had no choice but to follow.

The most direct route up to the mine was a treacherous path of loose shale. Jors slipped, slammed one knee into the ground, and somehow managed to catch himself before he slid all the way back to the bottom.

:Chosen? Are you hurt?:

Behind him, he could hear hooves scrabbling at the stone

and he had to grin. *:I'm fine, worrywart. Get back on solid ground before you do yourself some damage.:*

Here I go into who-knows-what to face a wounded mountain cat and he's worried that I've skinned my knee. Shaking his head, Jors struggled the rest of the way to the mine entrance, then turned and waved down at the glimmering white shape below. *:I'm here. I'm fine.:* Then he frowned and peered at the ground. The cart tracks coming out of the mine bumped down a series of jagged ledges, disappeared completely, then reappeared down where his Companion was standing.

:I don't like this.:

If he squinted, Jors could easily make out Gervis sidestepping nervously back and forth, a glimmer of white amidst the evening shadows. *:Hey, I don't like this either but…:*

:Something is going to happen.:

Jors chewed on his lip. He'd never heard his usually phlegmatic Companion sound so unsettled. A gust of wind blew cold rain in his face and he shivered. *:It's just a storm. Go back under the trees so you don't get soaked.:*

:No. Come down. We can come back here in the morning.:

The storm probably had him a bit spooked, and he didn't want to admit it. The Herald sighed and wished he could go along with his Companion's sudden change of mind. *:I can't do that.:* As much as he didn't want to go into that hole, he knew he had to. *:I wounded it. I can't let it die slowly, in pain. I'm responsible for its death.:*

He felt a reluctant agreement from below and, half wishing Gervis had continued to argue, turned to face the darkness. Setting his bow to one side, he pulled a small torch out of his pack, unwrapped the oilskin cover, and, in spite of wind and stiff fingers, got it lit.

The flame helped a little. But not much.

How was he supposed to hold a torch and aim a bow? This was ridiculous. But he'd missed his shot, and he couldn't let an animal, any animal, die in pain because of something he'd done.

The tunnel sloped gently back into the hillside, the shadows becoming more impenetrable the further from the entrance he went. He stepped over a fallen beam and a pile of rock, worked his way around a crazily angled corner, saw a smear of blood glistening in the torch light, and went on. His heart beat so loudly, he doubted he'd be able to hear the cat if it should turn and attack.

A low shadow caught his eye, and against his better judgement, he bent to study it. An earlier rockfall had exposed what looked to be the upper corner of a cave. In the dim, flickering light, he couldn't tell how far down it went, but a tossed rock seemed to fall forever.

The wind howled. He jumped, stumbled, and laughed shakily at himself. It was just the storm rushing past the entrance; he hadn't gone so far in that he wouldn't be able to hear it.

Then his torch blew out.

:Chosen!:

:No, it's okay. I'm all right.: His startled shout still echoed, bouncing back and forth inside the tunnels. *:I'm in the dark, but I'm okay.:* Again, he set his bow aside and pulled his tinderbox from his belt pouch with trembling fingers. *Get a grip, Jors*, he told himself firmly. *You're a Herald. Heralds are not afraid of the dark.*

And then the tunnel twisted. Flung to his knees and then his side, Jors wrapped his head in his arms and tried to present as small a target as possible to the falling rock. The earth heaved as though a giant creature deep below struggled to get free. With a deafening roar, a section of the tunnel collapsed. Lifted and slammed against a pile of rock, Jors lost track of up and down. The world became noise and terror and certain death.

Then half his body was suspended over nothing at all. He had a full heartbeat to realize what was happening before he fell, a large amount of loose rock falling with him.

It seemed to go on forever; turning, tumbling, sometimes sliding, knowing that no one could survive the eventual landing.

But he did. Although it took him a moment to realize it.

:Chosen! Jors! Chosen!:

:Gervis…: The near panic in his Companion's mindspeech pulled him up out of a grey and red blanket of pain, the need to reassure the young stallion delaying his own hysteria. *:I'm alive. Calm down, I'm alive.:* He spit out a mouthful of blood and tried to move.

Most of the rock that had fallen with him seemed to have landed on his legs. Teeth clenched, he flexed his toes inside his boots and almost cried in relief at the response. Although muscles from thigh to ankle spasmed, everything worked. *:I don't think I'm even hurt very badly.:* Which was true enough as far as it went. He had no way of telling what kind of injuries lurked under the masking pressure of the rock.

:I'm coming!:

:No, you're not!: He'd landed on his stomach, facing up a slope of about thirty degrees. He could lift his torso about a handspan. He could move his left arm freely. His right was pinned by his side. Breathing heavily, he rested his cheek

against the damp rock and closed his eyes. It made no difference to the darkness, but it made him feel better. *:Gervis, you're going to have to go for help. I can't free myself, and you can't get to me.:* He tried to envision his map, tried to trace the route they'd taken tracking the cat, tried to work out distances. *:There's a mining settlement closer than the farmstead, just follow the old mine trail, it should take you right to it.:*

:But you. . . .:

:I'm not going anywhere until you get back.:

"I'm not going anywhere," he repeated to the darkness as he felt the presence of his Companion move rapidly away. "I'm not going anywhere." Unfortunately, as the mountain pressed in on him, and all he could hear was his own terror filling the silence, that was exactly what he was afraid of.

* * *

It was hard to hear anything over the storm that howled around the chimneys and shutters, but Ari's ears were her only contact with the world, and she'd learned to sift sound for value. Head cocked, tangled hair falling over the ruin of her eyes, she listened. Rider coming. Galloping hard. She smiled, smug and silent. Not much went on that she didn't know about first. Something must've gone wrong somewhere. Only reason to be riding so hard in this kind of weather.

The storm had been no surprise, not with her stumps aching so for the past two days. She rubbed at them, hacking and spitting into the fire.

"Mama, Auntie Ari did it again."

"Hush, Robin. Leave her alone."

That's right, leave me alone. She spat once more, just because she knew the child would still be watching, then lifted herself on her palms and hand-walked towards her bench in the corner.

"Ari, can I get you something?"

Sometimes she thought they'd never learn. Grunting a negative, because ignoring them only brought renewed and more irritating offers, she swung herself easily up onto the low bench just as the pounding began. Sounded like they didn't even dismount. She couldn't wait.

"Who can it be at this hour?"

Her cousin, Dyril. *Answer it and find out, idiot.*

"Stone me, it's a horse!"

The sound of hooves against the threshold were unmistakable. She could hear the creak of leather harness, the snorting and blowing of an animal ridden hard, could even smell the hot scent of it from all the way across the room – but somehow it didn't add up to horse.

And while the noises it was making were certainly horse-like…

From the excited babble at the door, Ari managed to separate two bits of relevant information; the horse was riderless, and it was nearly frantic about something.

"What colour is it?"

It took a moment for Ari to recognize the rough and unfamiliar voice as her own. A stunned silence fell, and she felt the eyes of her extended family turned on her. Her chin rose, and her lips thinned. "Well?" she demanded, refusing to let them see she was as startled as they were. "What colour is it?"

"He's not a it, Auntie Ari, he's a he. And he's white. And his eyes are blue. And horses don't got blue eyes."

Young Robin was obviously smarter than she'd suspected.

"Of course they don't. It's not a horse, you rock-headed morons. Can't you recognize a Companion when you see one?"

The Companion made a sound that could only be agreement. As the babble of voices broke out again, Ari snorted and shook her head in disbelief.

"A Companion without a Herald?"

"Is it searching?"

"What happened to the Herald?"

Ari heard the Companion spin and gallop away, return and gallop away again.

"I think it wants us to follow it."

"Maybe its Herald is hurt and it's come here for help."

And did you figure that out all on your own? Ari rubbed at her stumps as various members of the family scrambled for jackets and boots and some of the children were sent to rouse the rest of the settlement.

When, with a great thunder of hooves, the rescue party galloped off, she beat her head lightly against the wall, trying not to remember.

"Auntie Ari?"

Robin. Made brave, no doubt, by her breaking silence. Well, she wouldn't do it again.

"Auntie Ari, tell me about Companions." He had a high-pitched, imperious little voice. "Tell me."

Tell him about Companions. Tell him about the time spent at the Collegium wishing her Blues were Grey. Tell him how the skills of mind and hand that had earned her a place seemed so suddenly unimportant next to the glorious honour of being Chosen. Tell him of watching them gallop across the Companion's field, impossibly beautiful, impossibly graceful

– infinitely far from her mechanical world of stresses and supports, and levers and gears.

Tell him how she'd made certain she was never in the village when the Heralds came through riding circuit, because it hurt so much to see such beauty and know she could never be a part of it. Tell him how, after the accident, she'd stuffed her fingers in her ears at the first sound of bridle bells.

Tell him any or all of that?

"You saw them, didn't you, Auntie Ari. You saw them up close when you were in the city."

"Yes." And then she regretted she'd said so much.

* * *

:Chosen! I've brought hands to dig you out.:

Jors released a long, shuddering breath that warmed the rock under his cheek and tried very, very hard not to cry.

:Chosen?:

The distress in his Companion's mindspeech helped him pull himself together. *:I'm okay. As okay as I was, anyway. I just, I just missed you.:* Gervis' presence settled gently into his mind, and he clung to it, more afraid of dying alone in the dark than of just dying.

:Do not think of dying.:

He hadn't realized he'd been thinking of it in such a way as to be heard. *:Sorry. I guess I'm not behaving much like a Herald, am I?:*

A very equine snort made him smile. *:You are a Herald, therefore this is how Heralds behave trapped in a mine.:*

The Companion's tone suggested he not argue the point, so he changed the subject. *:How did you manage to communicate with the villagers?:*

:When they recognized what I was, they followed me. Once they saw where you were, they understood. Some have returned to the village for tools.: He paused, and Jors had the feeling he was deciding whether or not to pass on one last bit of information. *:They call this place the Demon's Den.:*

:Oh, swell.:

:There are no real demons in it.:

:That makes me feel so much better.:

:It should,: Gervis pointed out helpfully.

* * *

"Herald's down in the Demon's Den." The storm swirled the voice in through the open door, stirring the room up into a frenzy of activity. All the able-bodied who hadn't followed the Companion ran for jackets and boots. The rest buzzed like a nest of hornets poked with a stick.

Ari sat in her corner, behind the tangled tent of her hair, and tried not to remember.

There was a rumble, deep in the bowels of the hillside, a warning of worse to come. But they kept working because Ari had braced the tunnels so cleverly that the earth could move as it liked and the mine would move with it, flexing instead of shattering.

But this time, the earth moved in a way she hadn't anticipated. Timbers cracked. Rock began to fall. Someone screamed.

* * *

Jors jerked his head up and hissed through his teeth in pain.

:Chosen?:

:I can hear them. I can hear them digging.: The distant sound of metal against stone was unmistakable.

Then it stopped.

:Gervis? What's wrong? What's happening?:

:Their lanterns keep blowing out. This hillside is so filled with natural passageways that when the winds are strong they can't keep anything lit.:

:And it's in an unstable area.: Jors sighed and rested his forehead against the back of his left wrist. *:What kind of an idiot would put a mine in a place like this?:*

:The ore deposits were very good.:

:How do you know?: Their familiar banter was all that was keeping him from despair.

:These people talk a great deal.:

:And you listen.: He clicked his tongue, knowing his Companion would pick up the intent if not the actual noise. *:Shame on you. Eavesdroppers never hear good of themselves.:*

Only the chime of a pebble, dislodged from somewhere up above answered.

:Gervis?:

:There was an accident.:

:Was anyone hurt?:

:I don't... No, not badly. They're coming out.:

He felt a rising tide of anger before he "heard" his Companion's next words.

"They're not going back in! I can't make them go back in! They say it's too dangerous! They say they need the light! I can't make them go back in.:

In his mind's eye, Jors could see the young stallion, rearing and kicking and trying to block the miners who were leaving him there to die. He knew it was his imagination, for their bond had never been strong enough for that kind of contact. He also knew his imagination couldn't be far wrong when the only answer to his call was an overwhelming feeling of angry betrayal.

The damp cold had crept through his leathers and begun to seep into his bones. He'd fallen just before full dark, and although time was hard to track buried in the hillside, it had to still be hours until midnight. Nights were long at this time of the year, and it would grow much, much colder before sunrise.

* * *

Ari knew, when Dyril and the others returned, that they didn't have the Herald with them. Knew it even before the excuses began.

"That little shake we had earlier was worse up there. What's left of the tunnels could go at any minute. We barely got Neegan out when one of the last supports collapsed."

"You couldn't get to him."

It wasn't a question. Not really. If they'd been able to get to him, they'd have brought him back.

"Him, her. We couldn't even keep the lanterns lit."

Someone tossed their gear to the floor. "You know what it's like up there during a storm; the wind howling through all those cracks and crevices…"

Ari heard Dyril sigh, heard wood creak as he dropped onto a bench. "We'll go back in the morning. Maybe when we can see…"

Memories were thick in the silence.

"If it's as bad as all that, the Herald's probably dead anyway."

"He's alive!" Ari shouted over the murmur of agreement. Oh sure, they'd feel better if they thought the Herald was dead, if they could convince themselves they hadn't left him there to die, but she wasn't going to let them off so easily.

"You don't know that."

"The Companion knows it!" She bludgeoned them with her voice because it was all she had. "He came to you for help!"

"And we did what we could! The Queen'll understand. The Den's taken too many lives already for us to throw more into it."

"Do you think I don't know that!" She could hear the storm throwing itself against the outside of the house but nothing from within. It almost seemed as though she were suddenly alone in the room. Then she heard a bench pushed back, footsteps approaching.

"Who else do you want that mine to kill?" Dyril asked quietly. "We lost three getting you out. Wasn't that enough?"

It was three too many, she wanted to say. If you think I'm grateful, think again. But the words wouldn't come. She swung down off her bench and hand-walked along the wall to the ladder in the corner. Stairs were difficult, but with only half a body to lift, she could easily pull herself, hand over hand, from rung to rung – her arms and shoulders were probably stronger now than they'd ever been. Adults couldn't stand in the loft, so no one bothered her there.

"We did all we could," she heard Dyril repeat wearily, more to himself than to her. She supposed she believed him. He was a good man. They were all good people. They wouldn't leave anyone to die if they had any hope of getting them out.

She'd been trapped with four others, deep underground. They could hear screaming, the sound carried on the winds that howled through the caves and passages around the mine.

By the time they could hear rescuers frantically digging with picks and shovels, there were only three of them still alive. Ari hadn't been able to feel her legs for some time, so when they'd pried enough rubble clear to get a rope through, she'd forced her companions out first. The Demon's Den had been her mine, and they were used to following her orders.

Then the earth had moved again, and the passage closed. She'd laid there, alone, listening to still more death carried on the winds and wishing she'd had the courage to tell them to leave her. To get out while they still could.

"Papa, what happened to the Companion?"

"He's still out there. Brandon tried to bring him into the stable and got a nasty bite for his trouble."

Ari moved across the loft to the narrow dormer and listened. Although the wind shrieked and whistled around the roof, she could hear the frenzied cries of the Companion as he pounded through the settlement, desperately searching for someone to help.

"Who else do you want that mine to kill?"

She dug through the mess on the floor for a leather strap, and tied her hair back off her face. Her jacket lay crumpled in a damp pile where she'd left it, but that didn't matter. It'd be damper still before she was done.

Down below, the common room emptied as the family headed for their beds, voices rising and falling, some needing comfort and absolution, some giving it. Ari didn't bother to listen. It didn't concern her.

Later, in the quiet, she swarmed down the ladder and hand-walked to where she'd heard the equipment dropped and sorted out a hundred-foot coil of rope. Draping it across her chest, she continued to the door. The latch was her design; her fingers remembered it.

The ground felt cold and wet under the heavy callouses

on her palms, and she was pretty sure she felt wet snow in amongst the rain that slapped into her face. She moved out away from the house and waited.

Hooves thundered past her, around her, and stopped.

"No one," she said, "knows the Den better than I do. I'm the only chance your Herald has left. You've probably called for others – other Heralds, other Companions – but they can't be close enough to help, or you wouldn't still be hanging around here. The temperature's dropping, and time means everything now."

The Companion snorted, a great gust of warm, sweetly scented breath replacing the storm for a moment. She hadn't realized he'd stopped so close, and she fought to keep from trembling.

"I know what you're thinking. But I won't need eyes in the darkness, and you don't dig with legs and feet. If you can get me there, Shining One, I can get your Herald out."

The Companion reared and screamed a challenge.

Ari held up her hands. "I know you understand me," she said. "I know you're more than you appear. You've got to believe me. I will get your Herald out.

"If you lie down, I can grab the saddle horn and the cantle and hold myself on between them." On a horse, it would never work. Even if she could lift herself on, she'd never stay in the saddle once it started to move; her stumps were too short for balance. But then, she wouldn't be having this conversation with a horse.

A single whicker, and a rush of displaced air as a large body went to the ground a whisker's distance from her.

Ari reached out, touched one silken shoulder, and worked her way back. *You must be desperate to be going along with this,* she thought bitterly. *Never mind. You'll see.* Mounting was easy. Staying in the saddle as the Companion rose to his feet was another thing entirely. Somehow, she managed it. "All right." A deep breath, and she balanced her weight as evenly as she could, stumps spread. "Go."

He leapt forward so suddenly he nearly threw her off. Heart in her throat, she clung to the saddle as his pace settled to an almost gentle rocking motion completely at odds with the speed she knew he had to be travelling. She could feel the night whipping by her, rain and snow stinging her face.

In spite of everything, she smiled. She was on a Companion. Riding a Companion.

It was over too soon.

* * *

:Jors? Chosen!:

The Herald coughed and lifted his head. He'd been having the worst dream about being trapped in a cave-in. That's what he got for eating his own cooking. And then he tried to move his legs and realized he wasn't dreaming. *:Gervis! You went away!:*

:I'm sorry, Heartbrother, please forgive me, but when they wouldn't stay...: The thought trailed off, lost in an incoherent mix of anger and shame.

:Hey, it's all right.: Jors carefully pushed his own terror back in order to reassure the Companion. *:You're back now, that's all that matters.:*

:I brought someone to get you out.:

:But I thought the mine was unstable, still collapsing.:

:She says she can free you.:

:You're talking to her?: As far as Jors knew, that never happened. Even some Heralds were unable to mindspeak clearly.

:She's talking to me. I believe she can do what she says.:

Jors swallowed and took a deep breath. *:No. It's too danger-ous. There's already been one accident. I don't want anyone dying because of me.:*

:Chosen…: The Companion's mental voice held a tone Jors had never heard before. *:I don't think she's doing it for you.:*

* * *

When they stopped, Ari took a moment to work some feeling back into each hand in turn. The Herald was going to have her finger marks permanently denting his gear. Below her, the Companion stood perfectly still, waiting.

"We're going to have to do this together, Shining One, because if I do it alone, I'll be too damned slow. Go past the mine about fifty feet and look up. Five, maybe six feet off the ground there should be a good, solid shelf of rock. If you can get us onto it, we can follow it right to the mouth of the mine and avoid all that shale shit."

The Companion whickered once and started walking. When she felt him turn, Ari scooted back as far as she could in the saddle, and flopped forward, trapping the coil of rope under her chest. Stretching her arms down and around the sleek curve of his barrel, she pushed the useless stirrups out of her way and clutched the girth.

"Go," she grunted.

He backed up a few steps, lunged forward, and the world tilted at a crazy angle.

Ari held her uncomfortable position until he stopped on the level ground at the mouth of the mine. "Remind me," she coughed, rubbing the spot where the saddle-horn had slammed into her throat, "not to do that again. All right, Shining One, I'll have to get off the same way I got on."

His movement took her by surprise. She grabbed for the saddle, her cold fingers slipped on the wet leather, and she dismounted a lot further from the ground than she'd intended.

A warm muzzle pushed into her face as she lay there for a moment, trying to get her breath back. "I'm okay," she muttered. "Just a little winded." Teeth gritted against the pain in her stumps, she pushed herself up.

Soft lips nuzzled at her hair.

"Don't worry, Shining One." Tentatively, she reached out and stroked the Companion's velvet nose. "I'll get your Herald out. There's enough of me left for that." She tossed her head and turned towards the mine, not needing eyes to find the gaping hole in the hillside. Icy winds dragged across her cheeks, and she knew by their touch that they'd danced through the Demon's Den before they came to her.

"Now then…" She was pleased to hear that her voice remained steady. "…we need to work out a way to communicate. At the risk of sounding like a bad Bardic tale, how about one whicker for yes and two for no?"

There was a single, soft whicker just above her head.

"Good. First of all, we have to find out how badly he…" A pause. "Your Herald is a he?" At the Companion's affirmative, she went on. "How badly he's hurt. Ask him if he has any broken bones."

* * *

:I don't know. I can't move enough to tell.:

* * *

Ari frowned at the answer. "Yes and no? Is he buried?"

* * *

:Only half of me.:
:Chosen, I have no way to tell her that.:
:Then yeah, I guess I'm buried.:

* * *

"Shit." There could be broken bones under the rock, the pressure keeping the Herald from feeling the pain. Well, she'd just have to deal with that when she got to it. "Is he buried in the actual mine, or in a natural cave?"

* * *

:She seems to think it's good you're in a natural cave.:
Jors traced the rock that curved away from him with his free hand. His fingers were so numb he could barely feel it. *:Why?:*
:I can't ask her that, Chosen. She wants to know if you turned left around a corner, about thirty feet in from the entrance to the mine.:
:Left?: He tried to remember, but the cold had seeped into his brain and thoughts moved sluggishly through it. *:I… I guess so.:*

* * *

"Okay." Ari tied one end of the rope around her waist as she spoke. "Ask him if the quake happened within, say twenty feet of that corner."

* * *

:I don't know. I don't remember. Gervis, I'm tired. Just stay with me while I rest.:
:No! Heartbrother do not go to sleep. Think, please, were you close to the corner?:

He remembered seeing the blood. Then stopping and looking into the hole in the side of the tunnel. *:Yes. I think no more than twenty feet.:*

* * *

"Good. We're in luck, there's only one place on this level where the cave system butts up against the mine. I know approximately where he is. He's close." She reached forward and sifted a handful of rubble. "I just have to get to him."

A hundred feet of rope would reach the place where the quake threw him out of the mine, but after that, she could only hope he hadn't slid too deep into the catacombs.

Turning to where she could feel the bulk of the Companion, Ari's memory showed her a graceful white stallion, outlined against the night. "Once I get the rope around him, you'll have to pull him free."

He whickered once and nudged her, and she surrendered to the urge to bury face and fingers in his mane. When she finally let go, she had to bite her lip to keep from crying. "Thanks. I'm okay now."

Using both arms at once, then swinging her body forward between them, Ari made her way into the mine, breathing in the wet, oily scent of the rock, the lingering odours of the lanterns Dyril and the others had used, and the stink of fear, old and new. At the first rockfall she paused, traced the broken pieces, and found the passage the earlier rescue party had dug.

Her shoulder brushed a timber support, and she hurried past the memories.

A biting gust of wind whistled through a crack up ahead, flinging grit up into her face. "Nice try," she muttered. "But you threw me into darkness five years ago, and I've learned my way around." Then she raised her voice. "Shining One, can you still hear me?"

The Companion's whicker echoed eerily.

"You don't need to worry about him running out of air, this place is like a sieve, so remind your Herald to keep moving. Tell him to keep flexing his muscles if that's all he can do. He's got to keep the blood going out to the extremities."

* * *

:What extremities?: Jors heard himself giggle, and wondered what there was to laugh about.

:Chosen, listen to me. You know what the cold can do. You have to move.:

:I know that.: Everyone knew that. It wasn't like he hadn't been paying attention when they'd been teaching winter survival skills, it was just, well, it was just so much effort.

:Wiggle your toes!:

Gervis somehow managed to sound exactly like the Weaponsmaster, and Jors found himself responding instinctively. To his surprise, his toes still wiggled. And it still hurt. The pain burned some of the frost out of his brain and left him gasping for breath, but he was thinking more clearly than he had been in some time. With his Companion's encouragement, he began to systematically work each muscle that still responded.

* * *

The biggest problem with digging out the Demon's Den had always been that the rock shattered into pieces so small it was like burrowing through beads in a box. The slightest jar would send the whole crashing to the ground.

Her eyes in her fingertips, Ari inched towards the buried Herald, not digging but building a passageway, each stone placed exactly to hold the weight of the next. Slowly, with exquisite care, she moved up and over the rockfall that had nearly killed Neegan. She lightly touched the splintered end of the shattered support, then went on. She had no time to mourn the past.

Years of destruction couldn't erase her knowledge of the mine. She'd been trapped in it for too long.

* * *

"Herald? Can you hear me?"

Jors turned his face towards the sudden breeze. "Yes…" *:Gervis, she's here!:*

:Good.: Although he sounded relieved, Jors realized the Companion didn't sound the least bit surprised.

:You knew she'd make it.:

Again the strange tone the Herald didn't recognize. *:I believed her when she said she'd get you out.:*

"Cover your head with your hands, Herald."

Startled, he curved his left arm up and around his head just in time to prevent a small shower of stones from ringing off his skull.

"I'm on my way down."

A moment later, he felt the space around him fill, and a rough jacket pressed hard against his cheek.

"Sorry. Just let me get turned."

Turned? Teeth chattering from the cold, he strained back as far as he could, but knew it would make little difference. There wasn't room for a cat to turn, let alone a person. To his astonishment, his rescuer seemed to double back on herself.

"Ow. Not a lot of head room down here."

From the sound of her voice and the touch of her hands, she had to be sitting tight up against his side, her upper body bent across his back. He tried to force his half-frozen mind to work. "Your legs…"

"Are well out of the way, Herald. Trust me." Ari danced her fingers over the pile of rubble that pinned him. "Can you still move your toes."

It took him a moment to remember how. "Yes."

"Good. You're at the bottom of a roughly wedge-shaped crevice. Fortunately, you're pointing the right way. As soon as I get enough of you clear, I'm going to tie this rope around you, and your Companion on the other end is going to inch you up the slope as I uncover your legs. That means if anything's broken it's going to drag, but if we don't do it that way there won't be room down here for me, you, and the rock. Do you understand?"

"Yes."

"Good." One piece at a time she began to free his right side.

:Gervis, she doesn't have any legs.:

:I know.:

:How did she get here?:

:I brought her.:

:That's impossible!:

The Companion snorted. :Obviously not. She's blind, too.:

"What!" His incredulous exclamation echoed through the Demon's Den.

Ari snorted and jammed a rock into the crack between two others. It wasn't difficult to guess what had caused that reaction, not when she knew the silence had to be filled with dialogue she couldn't hear. She waited for him to say something Herald-like and nauseating about overcoming handicaps as though they were all she was.

To her surprise, he said only, "What's your name?"

It took her a moment to find her voice. "Ari."

"Jors."

She nodded, even though she knew he couldn't see the gesture. "Herald Jors."

"Are you one of the miners?"

Why was he talking to her when he had his Companion to keep him company? "Not exactly." So far tonight, she'd said more than she'd said in the five years since the accident. Her throat ached.

"Gervis says he's never seen anyone do what you did to get in here. He says you didn't dig through the rubble, you built a tunnel around you, using nothing but your hands."

"Gervis?"

"My Companion. He's very impressed. He believes you can get me out."

Ari swallowed hard. His Companion believed in her. It was almost funny, in a way. "You can move your arm now."

"Actually," he gasped, trying not to writhe, "no I can't." He felt her reach across him, tuck her hand under his chest, and grab his wrist. He could barely feel her touch against his skin.

"On three." She pulled immediately before he could tense.

"That wasn't very nice," he grunted when he could speak again.

She ignored his feeble attempt to tug his arm out of her hands and continued rubbing life back into the chilled flesh. "There's nothing wrong with it. It's just numb because you've been lying on it in the cold."

"Oh? Are you a Healer then?"

He sounded so indignant that she smiled, and actually answered the question. "No, I was a mining engineer. I designed this mine."

"Oh." He'd wondered what kind of idiot would put a mine in a place like this. Now, he knew.

Ari heard most of the thought and gritted her teeth. "Keep flexing the muscles." Untying the end of the rope from around her own waist, she retied it just under the Herald's arms. It felt strange to touch a young man's body again after so long. Strange and uncomfortable. She twisted and began to free his legs.

Jors listened to her breathing and thought of being alone in darkness forever.

:I'm here, Chosen.:

:I know. But I wasn't thinking of me. I was thinking about Ari… Ari…: "Were you at the Collegium?"

"I was."

"You redesigned the hoists from the kitchen, so they'd stop jamming. And you fixed that pump in Bardic that kept flooding the place. And you made the practise dummy that…"

"That was a long time ago."

"Not so long," Jors protested, trying to ignore the sudden pain as she lifted a weight off his hips. "You left the Blues the year I was Chosen."

"Did I?"

"They were all talking about you. They said there wasn't anything you couldn't build. What happened?"

Her hands paused. "I came home. Be quiet. I have to listen." It wasn't exactly a lie.

Working as fast as she could, Ari learned the shape of the stone imprisoning the Herald, its strengths, its weaknesses.

It was all so very familiar. The tunnel she'd built behind her ended here. She finished it in her head, and nodded, once, as the final piece slid into place.

"Herald Jors, when I give you the word have your Companion pull gently, but firmly on the rope until I tell you to stop. I can't move the rest of this off of you so I'm going to have to move you out from under it."

Jors nodded, realized how stupid that was, and said, "I understand."

Ari pushed her thumbs under the edge of a rock and took a deep breath. "Now."

The rock shifted, but so did the Herald.

"Stop." She changed her grip. "Now." A stone fell. She blocked it with her shoulder. "Stop."

Inch by inch, teeth clenched against the pain of returning circulation, Jors moved up the slope, clinging desperately to the rope.

"Stop."

"I'm out."

"I know. Now, listen carefully because this is important. On my way in, I tried to lay the rope so it wouldn't snag, but your Companion will have to drag you clear without stopping – one long smooth motion, no matter what."

"No matter what?" Jors repeated, twisting to peer over his shoulder, the instinctive desire to see her face winning out over the reality. The loose slope he was lying on shifted.

"Hold still!" Ari snapped. "Do you want to bury yourself again?"

Jors froze. "What's going to happen, Ari?"

Behind him, in the darkness, he heard her sigh. "Do you know what a keystone is, Herald?"

"It's the stone that takes the weight of the other stones and holds up the arch."

"Essentially. The rock that fell on your legs fell in such a way as to make it the keystone for this cavern we're in."

"But you didn't move the rock."

"No, but I did move your legs and they were part of it."

"Then what's supporting the keystone?" He knew before she answered.

"I am."

"No."

"No what, Herald?"

"No. I won't let you sacrifice your life for mine."

"Yet Heralds are often called upon to give their lives for others."

"That's different."

"Why?" Her voice cracked out of the darkness like a whip. "You're allowed to be noble, but the rest of us aren't? You're so good and pure and perfect and Chosen, and the rest of us don't even have lives worth throwing away? Don't you see how stupid that is? Your life is worth infinitely more than mine!" She stopped and caught her breath on the edge of a sob. "There should never have been a mine here. Do you know why I dug it? To prove I was as good as all those others who were Chosen when I wasn't. I was smarter. I wanted it as much. Why not me? And do you know what my pride did, Herald? It killed seventeen people when the mine collapsed. And then my cowardice killed my brother and an uncle and woman barely out of girlhood because I was afraid to die. My life wasn't worth all those lives. Let my death be worth your life at least."

He braced himself against her pain. "I can't let you die for me."

"And yet if our positions were reversed, you'd expect me to let you die for me." She ground the words out through the shards of broken bones, of broken dreams. "Heralds die for what they believe in all the time. Why can't I?"

"You've got it wrong, Ari," he told her quietly. "Heralds die, I won't deny that. And we all know we may have to sacrifice ourselves someday for the greater good. But we don't die for what we believe in. We live for it."

Ari couldn't stop shaking, but it wasn't from the cold or even from the throbbing pain in her stumps.

"Who else do you want that mine to kill?"

"This, all this, is my responsibility. I won't let it kill anyone else."

Because he couldn't reach her with his hands, Jors put his heart in his voice and wrapped it around her. "Neither will I. What will happen if you grab my legs and Gervis pulls us both free?"

He heard her swallow. "The tunnel will collapse."

"All at once?"

"No..."

"It'll begin here and follow us?"

"Yes. But not even a Companion could pull us out that quickly."

:Gervis...: Jors sketched the situation. *:Do you think you can beat the collapse?:*

:Yes, but do you think you can survive the trip? You'll be dragged on your stomach through a rock tunnel.:

:Well, I'm not going to survive much longer down here, that's for certain — I'm numb from my neck to my knees. I'm in leathers. I should be okay.:

:What about your head?:

:Good point.: "Ari, you're wearing a heavy sheepskin coat, can you work part of it up over your head?"

"Yes, but…"

"Do it. And watch for falling rock. I'm going to do the same."

"What about your pack?"

He'd forgotten all about it. Letting the loop of rope under his armpits hold his weight, he managed to secure it like a kind of crude helmet.

"Grab hold of my ankles, Ari."

"I…"

"Ari, I can't force you to live. I can only ask you not to die."

He felt a tentative touch, and then a firmer hold.

:Go, Gervis!:

* * *

They stayed at the settlement for nearly a week. Although the Healer assured him that the hours spent trapped in the cold and the damp had done no permanent damage, Jors wore a stitched cut along his jaw as a remembrance of the passage out of the Demon's Den.

Ari was learning to live again. She still carried the weight of the lives lost to her pride, but she'd found the strength to bear the load.

"Don't expect sweetness and light though," she cautioned the Herald as he and Gervis prepared to leave. "I was irritating and opinionated before the accident." Her mouth crooked slightly, and she added, with just a hint of the old bitterness, "I expect that's why I was never Chosen."

Jors grinned as Gervis pushed his head into her shoulder. "He says you were chosen for something else."

"He said that?" Ari lifted her hand and lightly stroked the Companion's face. She smiled, the expression feeling strange and new. "Then I guess I'd better get on with it."

As they were riding out of the settlement to take up their interrupted circuit again, Jors turned back to wave and saw Ari sketching something wondrous in the air, prodded by the piping questions of young Robin.

:I guess she won't be alone in the dark anymore.:

Gervis tossed his head. *:She never had to be.:*

:Sometimes it's hard for people to realize that.: They rode in silence for a moment, then Jors sighed, watching his breath plume in the frosty air. *:I'm glad they found the body of that cat – I'd hate to have to go back into the Den to look for it.:* Their route would take them nowhere near the mine. *:That was as close to the Havens as I want to come for a while.:* And then he realized.

:Gervis, you knew Ari wanted to die down there!:

:Yes.:

:Then why did you let her go into that mine?:

:Because I believed she could free you.:

:But…:

:And,: the Companion continued, *:I believed you could free her.:*

BROCK

Id's just a code."

Trying not to smile at the same protest he'd heard for the last two days, Jors set the empty mug on a small table. "Healer Lorrin says it's more, Isabel. She says you're spending the next two days in bed."

The older Herald tried to snort, but her nose had filled past the point it where was possible, and she had to settle for an avalanche of coughing instead. "She cud heal me," she muttered when she could finally breathe again.

"She seems to think that a couple of days in bed and a couple of hundred cups of tea will heal you just fine."

"Gibbing children their Greens…"

That was half a protest at best, and as Jors watched, Isabel's eyes closed, the lines exhaustion had etched around them beginning to ease. Leaning forward, he blew out the lamp, then quietly slipped from the room.

*

"Oh, she's sick," the Healer assured him, exasperation edging her voice. "What could have possessed her to ride courier at her age, at this time of the year? Yes, the package and information she brought from the Healer's Collegium will save lives this winter, but *surely* there had to have been younger Heralds around to deliver it?"

Jors opened his mouth to answer.

Lorrin gave him no chance. "If she hadn't run into you riding sector, she might not have made it this far. She needs rest, and I'm keeping her in bed until I think she's had enough of it."

Jors didn't argue. He wouldn't have minded an actual conversation – Lorrin was young and pretty – but unfortunately, she seemed too determined to run this new House of Healing the way she felt a House of Healing *should* be run to waste time in dalliance with the healthy.

*

"Have you good as new. You see. Good as new. Soft and clean."

Jors stopped just inside the stable door and stared in astonishment at the young man grooming his Companion. The stubby fingers that held the brush, the bulky body, the round face, angled eyes, and full mouth told the Herald that this unexpected groom was one of those the country people called Moonlings. He wore patched homespun; the pants too large, the shirt too small, both washed out to a grimy grey. His boots had seen at least one other pair of feet.

He'd already groomed the chirras and Isabel's Companion, Calida – the sleeping mare all but glowed in the dim stable light.

:Gervis?:

:His name is Brock.: The stallion's mental voice sounded sleepy and sated. *:Can we take him with us?:*

:No. And how do you know what his name is?:

:He talks to us and he knows exactly – oh, yes – where to rub.:

Companions were not in the habit of allowing themselves to be groomed by other than Heralds' hands. Jors found it hard to believe that they'd not only allowed Brock's ministrations, but were actually reveling in them. He stepped forward, and at the sound of his footfall, Brock turned.

His face broke into a broad smile, radiating welcome. Arms spread, he rushed at the Herald and wrapped him in a tight hug. Staring up at Jors, their faces barely inches apart, he joyfully repeated "Brother Herald!" over and over while a large grey dog leapt around them, barking.

:Gervis?:

:The dog's name is Rock. He's harmless.:

:Glad to hear that.:

"Brock… I can't breathe…"

"Sorry! Sorry." Releasing him so quickly Jors stumbled and had to grab the edge of a hay rack, Brock shuffled back, still smiling. "Sorry. I brushed." One short-fingered hand gestured back at the Companions. "Good as new. Soft and clean."

"You did a very good job." Jors stepped around the dog, now lying panting on the floor, and ran his fingers down Gervis' side. There wasn't a bit of straw, a speck of dust, a hair out of place on either Companion.

:Better than very good,: Gervis sighed.

Jors smiled and repeated the compliment. *:Did you say thank you, you fuzzy hedonist?:*

In answer, the Companion stretched out his neck and gently nuzzled Brock's cheek, receiving a loud, smacking kiss in return.

"Okay. We go now." Brock bent and picked a ragged, grey sweater out of the straw and wrestled it over his head. "We go *now,*" he repeated, placing both hands in the small of Jors' back and pushing him toward the stable door. "Or we come late and Mister Mayor is mad and yells."

"Late for…?"

"The petitions.: Gervis' mental voice sounded more than a little amused, and Jors remembered he'd intended to merely look in on the Companions on his way to the town hall.

Heading out into the square, he realized Brock was trotting to keep up, and he shortened his stride. "Does the mayor yell a lot?"

"Yes. A lot."

"Do you know why?"

Brock sighed deeply, one hand dropping to fondle the ears of the dog walking beside him. "Mister Mayor wears the town," he said very seriously after a moment. "The town swings heavy heavy."

Okay; that made no sense. Maybe we should try something less complex. "Is Rock your dog?"

"He's my friend. They were hurting him. I… Wait!"

Uncertain of just who had been told to wait, Jors watched Brock and the dog run across to the town well where a pair of women argued over who'd draw their water first. Ignored in the midst of the argument, Brock began to draw water for them. He had no trouble with the winch, but while pouring from bucket to bucket, he splashed the older woman's skirt. Suddenly united, they turned on him. By the time Jors arrived, Brock had filled another bucket in spite of the shouting – although his shoulders were hunched forward and he didn't look happy.

The older woman saw him first, shoved the other, and the shouting stopped.

"Ladies."

"Herald," they said in ragged unison.

"Let me give you a hand with that, Brock. You bring the water up, and I'll pour."

"Pouring is hard," Brock warned.

"Herald, you don't have to," one of the women protested. "We never asked this…" When Jors turned a bland stare in her direction, she reconsidered her next word. "…boy to help."

"I know." His tone cut off any further protests, and neither woman said anything until all the buckets had been filled, then they thanked him far more than the work he'd done required. He'd turned to go when, at the edge of his vision, he saw one woman lean forward and pinch Brock on the arm, hissing, "Now that's a *real* Herald."

"HERALD JORS!"

Across the square, the mayor stood on the steps of the town hall, chain of office glinting in the pale autumn sunlight, both hands urging him to hurry. *Well, he'll just have to wait!* Lips pressed into a thin line, Jors turned back toward the well, had his elbow firmly grabbed, and found himself facing the mayor again.

"Mister Mayor is yelling," Brock explained, moving Jors across the square.

"Let him. I saw what happened back there. I saw that woman pinch you."

"Yes." He threw a satisfied smile toward Jors, never lessening their forward motion. "I made them stop fighting. Heralds do that."

"Yes, they do." They'd almost reached the hall, and Jors had a strong suspicion that digging his heels in would have had no effect. "You're stronger than you look."

"Have to be."

I'll bet, Jors thought as he caught sight of the mayor's expression.

"Brock! Get your filthy hands off that Herald!"

"Hands are clean."

"I don't care! He doesn't need you hanging around him!"

"I don't mind." Jors swept through the door, Brock caught up in his wake, both moving too quickly for the mayor to do anything but fall in behind.

"Heralds work together," Brock announced proudly. He clapped his hands as heads began to turn. "Be in a good line now. Heralds are here."

"Heralds?" a male voice jeered from the crowd. "I see only one Herald, Moonling."

"Heralds!" Brock repeated, throwing his arms around Jors' waist in another hug. "Me and him."

:Oh, Havens.:

:Trouble, Heartbrother?:

:I just realized something that should have been obvious — Brock believes he's a Herald.:

:So? You'd rather he believed he was a pickpocket?:

:That's not the point.:

But he couldn't let the townspeople chase Brock from

the hall as they clearly wanted to do, and Brock wouldn't leave because it was time for the Heralds to hear petitions, so Jors ended up sitting him at the table and hoping for the best.

He realized his mistake early on. Brock had a loudly expressed opinion on everything, up to and including calling one of the petitioners a big fat liar – which turned out to be true; on all points. Unfortunately, short of having him physically carried out of the hall, Jors could think of no way to get him to leave. *:Have him check on Isabel.:*

:How…?:

:You're worried. You're projecting. And I'm only across the square. If he wants to be with a Herald, send him to check on Isabel. She's sick, and she needs company.:

:That's a terrific idea.:

Gervis' mental voice sounded distinctly smug. *:I know.:*

It worked. Jors only wished the Companion had thought of it sooner. A Herald's office protected him or her from the repercussions of a judgment – no matter how disgruntled the losing petitioner might be, few would risk the grave penalties attached to attacking a Herald. Brock didn't have that protection.

*

"No, Brock's not here." Healer Lorrin continued rolling strips of soft linen. "He left at sunset for the tavern."

"The tavern?"

"He's there every evening. He fills their wood box, and they feed him. Him and Rock."

"He works there?"

Lorrin nodded. "There, and the blacksmith's, whenever

there's a nervy horse in to be shoed. Animals trust him. I tried to have him deliver teas to patients, but if he's carrying something, there's always troublemakers who try to take it from him."

"I'm surprised." Jors rubbed his elbow at the memory. "He's quite strong."

"Is he?" She set the finished roll with the others and picked up a new strip of cloth. "He's bullied all the time, but I've never seen him defend himself. Did you know that poorer mothers have him watch their infants if they have to leave them? I'll tell you something, Herald. When I came here, I was amazed to discover this town has almost none of those horrible accidents that happen when a baby just starting to creep is left alone and burns to death or drowns – that's because of Brock."

"Where does he sleep?" This far north, the nights were already cold.

"In various stables when the weather's good. By someone's hearth when it isn't."

"Has he no family?"

"His parents were old when he was born. Old and poor. They died about three years ago and left him nothing."

"Why doesn't someone take him in?"

"He doesn't want to be taken," the Healer snapped. "He's not a stray cat, and for all he can be childlike, he's not a child. He's a grown man, probably not much younger than you, and he has the same right as you do to choose his life."

"But…"

She sighed and her tone softened. "There are those who try to make sure he doesn't suffer for those choices, but that's all anyone has a right to do. Besides…" One corner of her mouth quirked up. "…he tells me that Heralds never stay in one place so no one thinks they like some people more than others."

Simpler language, but pretty much the official reason, Jors allowed. "How long has he believed himself to be a Herald?"

"As long as I've been here. I'm surprised you haven't heard about him from other Heralds. You can't be the first he's latched on to."

"He wasn't in the reports I read, and I…" About to say he doubted Brock would come up in casual conversation between Heralds, he frowned at a distinct feeling of unease. "I should go now."

"There's no need to go to the Waystation tonight, I've plenty of room." Her smile edged toward invitation. "I doubt anyone will accuse you of favouritism if you stay here."

"No. Thank you. I need to…" The feeling was growing stronger. "…Um, go."

He doubted she'd be smiling that way at him again, but personal problems were unimportant next to his growing certainty that something was wrong. Taking the steps two at a time, he hit the ground floor running and headed for the stables. *:Gervis?:*

:We can feel it, too. Calida says it's close.:

It wasn't in the stables or the corral, but when Jors opened the small door, a pair of huddled figures tumbled inside.

Brock lifted a tear-drenched face up from matted grey fur and wailed, "Heralds don't cry."

"Says who?" Jors demanded, dropping to one knee.

"People. When I cry."

"People are wrong. I'm a Herald and I cry." He stretched out a hand, keeping half his attention on the big dog, who watched him warily. Herald's Whites meant nothing to Rock, and he didn't lower his hackles until Gervis whickered a warning of his own. "What happened? Did someone hurt you?"

"Heralds don't tattle!"

His various tormentors had probably been telling him that for years. "If someone does something bad, we do."

"No."

"Yes. If we can't make it right on our own, we tell someone who can. Bad things should never be hidden. It makes them worse."

Brock drew in a long shuddering breath and slowly held out his arm. Below the ragged cuff of his sweater was a dark bruise where a large hand had gripped his wrist.

"Is that all?"

"Rock came. The man ran away."

"Who was it?"

"A bad man."

No argument there. "Do you know his name?"

"A bad man," Brock repeated, wiping his nose against the dog's shoulder.

:You catch him, and I'll kick him.: The Companion's mental voice was a near growl. *:Calida says she'll help.:*

*

"It's a bad bruise, but it is just a bruise. Healer Lorrin wrapped it in a herb pack, and she says he'll be fine." Jors ran both hands back through his hair. "He won't stay, says he's not sick enough, but I can't just let him wander off into the night."

"Coors you cand."

"And I can't take him to the Waystation, and I can't stay with him because that would be seen as losing impartiality. So, do you mind if he spends the night with Calida?"

Isabel managed a truncated snort. "Fine wid me, bud you'd bezd ask her."

*

Leading Gervis and the chirras out of the stable, Jors turned for one last look at Brock curled up against Calida's side. The elderly mare had been pleased to have the company and had positioned herself in such a way that Brock could pillow his head against her flank. Rock had snuggled up on the young man's other side, and although his face was still blotchy, Jors had never seen anyone look so completely at peace.

:Why do you two care about him so much?: he asked his Companion as he mounted.

:He believes he is a Herald.:

:Yes, but…:

:And he acts accordingly.:

*

The next day during petitions, the mayor tripped over Rock, sprawled by the table. Jerking his chain of office down into place, he snarled, "That dog is vicious and ought to be destroyed."

Jors pushed Brock back into his chair. "Who says this dog is vicious?"

The mayor's lip curled. "I heard he attacked a man last night."

"I heard that, too, Herald," called out one of the waiting petitioners.

"Brock, show everyone your arm." The bruises were dark and ugly against the pale skin. "The man Rock attacked did that and would have done more had the dog not come to his master's defense. This dog is no more vicious than I am."

"We've only your word on that, Herald. You can't truth-spell a dog."

"No, but I *can* truth-spell the man who made the accusation if he's willing to come forward."

No one was surprised when he didn't.

Mid-afternoon, as Jors was returning to the hall after a privy break, the town clerk fell into step beside him and apologized for the mayor's earlier behaviour. "It's just he feels responsible for the whole town, and it weighs on him and makes him short-tempered. Believe me, Herald, he's a whole different man when he can take that chain off."

"Mister Mayor wears the town. The town swings heavy heavy."
Brock's explanation suddenly made perfect sense.

*

It had been arranged that Brock would spend another night with Calida.

"Companions need Heralds. Lady Herald is sick. *I* am not sick. I am here." He threw his arms around Jors. "I see you tomorrow, Brother Herald."

"No, not tomorrow, Brock. Tomorrow, I'm going to see the tanners." Tanning was a smelly business, so tanners set up their pits downwind of towns – far enough away they could work without complaint, but not so far they couldn't get skins or find buyers for their hides. These particular tanners had chosen distance over convenience and had settled nearly a full day's travel away. The townspeople he'd spoken to about them had made it quite clear that the animosity was mutual. No one went near the place unless they had to. "I'll stay overnight, then go back to the Waystation the next day. The day after that, I'll be back in town. That's why I brought my chirras in today, so he won't be left alone at the station."

"No."

"It's okay. Gervis travels very fast, I won't be gone long."

"No!" Brock released him, stepping back just far enough to meet Jors' eyes. "Don't go!" Pulling the hair back off his face with one hand, he grabbed the Herald's wrist with the other. "See?" An old scar ran diagonally from the edge of a thick eyebrow up into his hairline.

"The tanners did that?"

"I bumped mean lady's cart. Don't go." His eyes welled over. "Mean lady is there."

Jors pulled free of Brock's grip and squeezed his shoulder. "I'll be fine. Really. The mean lady won't do anything to me." The sort of people who'd strike a frightened Moonling were unlikely to be the sort who'd strike a healthy young man in Herald's Whites. "But I have to go and check on them. They haven't been into town for a long time, and it's almost winter."

"Not alone."

"Don't worry, I'll have Gervis." He gave the trembling shoulder another squeeze then swung himself up into the saddle. "You stay with Calida, and I'll see you in two days."

He supposed he'd been half expecting it. When Jors came out of the Waystation early the next morning, there sat Brock – which was the half he supposed he'd been expecting – on Calida – which was a total surprise. It wasn't often a Companion would choose to bear anyone but her Chosen, and the exceptions were almost always Heralds.

"Good morning, Brother Herald!"

Actual Heralds. "Brock, what are you doing here?"

The young man's crestfallen expression insisted on better manners. Jors rubbed a hand over his face and sighed. "Good morning, Brock."

The smile returned. "It's early!"

"Yes, it is. What are you doing here so early?"

"I go with you. To tanners."

"No, you don't."

"Yes, I go with you."

"No. "

"Yes."

Jors hated to do it, but… "What about the mean lady?" The smile faltered as Brock sucked in his lower lip. "You don't want to see the mean lady."

"Don't want you to see mean lady alone." He took a deep breath and squared his shoulders. "I go with you."

"That's very brave of you." And he meant that. Courage was only courage in the face of fear. "But even though I know you mean well, you can't just *take* a Companion."

Brock's eyes widened indignantly. "Didn't take!"

:Calida says if she hadn't wanted him to ride her, he wouldn't be here.: Gervis scratched his cheek on a post and added thoughtfully. *:He's very bad at it.:*

:At what?:

:Riding.:

:No doubt. What does Isabel say about this?:

:Herald Isabel trusts her Companion.:

:That's not very helpful.:

:It should be.:

One more try. "Brock, by taking her Companion, you've left Herald Isabel alone."

"No." He leaned carefully forward in the saddle and stroked Calida's neck. "Left Rock."

Jors reached for Calida's bridle, but the Companion tossed her head, moving it away from his hand. "Calida, you *have* to take him back."

The mare gave him a flat, uncompromising stare.

:She says, "Make me.": Gervis translated helpfully.

:Yeah. I got that. What do you think I should do?:

:Help him down.:

:You think this is funny, don't you?: Jors demanded doing as the Companion suggested.

:I think this is inevitable, Chosen. You might as well make the best of it.:

Even with Jors' help, Brock stumbled as he hit the ground, fell, rolled, and bounced up, declaring, "I'm okay!"

:Now, get ready.: Gervis shoved at Jors' bare shoulder. *:We'll be moving slowly, and Calida says it's going to rain.:*

:And won't that make this a perfect day?:

:No. She says it's going to rain hard, and I don't like to get wet. I want to be there before it rains.:

That began to look more and more unlikely as the morning passed and the clouds grew darker. Brock managed to stay in the saddle at a fast walk, and Calida refused to go faster. Once or twice, Jors was positive he was going to fall off, but at the last instant he'd shift weight and somehow stay mounted.

:His balance is bad. But Calida's helping.:

:Why is Calida doing this?:

One ear flicked back. *:So he won't fall off.:*

:No, I mean why is Calida allowing any of this? Why is she allowing Brock to ride her? Why is she allowing, no, insisting he come along today?:

:She has her reasons.:

Jors sighed. He knew that tone. *:And you're not going to tell me what those reasons are, are you?:*

:He's very happy.:

:I can see that.:

Happy was an understatement. For all he held the pommel in a death grip, Brock looked ecstatic. *This is really not helping his delusion that he's a Herald,* Jors realized. Something would have to be done about that, and since the two of them were spending what was likely to be a full day traveling together, now would be the time to do it. Maybe *that* was why Calida had brought him.

There'd be no point in bluntly saying, *"Brock, you're not a Herald."* The townspeople said that all the time, shaded in every possible emotion from amusement to rage, and it had no effect.

"Brock, do you know what makes a person a Herald?"

"Heralds help people. Heralds can cry. Heralds tell when bad things happen." He beamed proudly. "I remember the new things."

"Yes, all those things make a Herald, but…"

"I'm a good Herald."

"…but there's other things."

Brock twisted in the saddle to look at him, and Calida adjusted her gait to prevent a fall. "Heralds wear shiny white."

"Yes…"

He looked down at his grey sweater, then looked back at Jors, smiling broadly. "Clothes are on the outside."

:And a Herald is on the inside.:

:I get it.:

A sapphire eye rolled back at him, distinctly amused. *:Just trying to help.:*

"Brock, all those things are part of being a Herald, but the most important part is being Chosen by a Companion. You don't have to be a Herald to be a really good person, but you *do* have to be Chosen. Do you understand?"

Brock nodded. "Companions have Heralds."

"*You* don't have a Companion."

"Yes!" He bounced indignantly, lost a stirrup, and nearly went off. "Have Calida," he continued when he was secure in the saddle again.

"But she's Herald Isabel's Companion. Herald Isabel is letting you ride her."

"No. Calida is letting."

:He's got you there.:

Jors sighed. "Riding a Companion isn't the point, Brock. You're not Calida's Herald."

"Not her Herald," Brock agreed, his smile lighting up his whole face. "A Herald."

Between the less-than-successful conversation and the glowering sky, Jors had picked up a pounding headache. They rode without speaking for a while, Brock humming tunelessly to himself. Finally, more to put an end to the humming than for any real desire to know, Jors turned in the saddle and said, "So, you were going to tell me how you saved Rock."

"Kids were hurting him." Brock's placid expression turned fierce at the memory. "I made them stop." Although he wouldn't defend himself, he seemed quite capable of defending the helpless. "He was hungry. I counted his bones. One, two, three, four…"

"Where did he come from?" Jors interrupted, unsure of how high the other man could count and not really wanting to find out.

"Don't know. Now, he is my friend." The broad brow furrowed as he searched for words. "Some mean people aren't mean now because he is my friend."

That was hardly surprising. Rock was a big dog. Probably a hunting dog of some kind, who'd gotten separated from his pack and managed to finally find his way back to people. "Why did you call him Rock?"

"So when kids are mean, it doesn't matter."

"I don't understand."

Brock stared down between Calida's ears and chanted, "Brock, Brock, dumb as a rock." Then he grinned and turned just far enough in the saddle to meet Jors' gaze. "Rock isn't dumb. I fooled them."

He looked so proud, Jors found himself grinning in return. "Yes, you did. That was very smart."

"I am a smart Herald."

It was a good thing he didn't need affirmation, because Jors had no idea of what to say. *:And now,:* he sighed quietly as large drops of cold water began splashing against his leathers, *:it's raining.:*

:I know. I'm getting wet.:

:So am I.:

:I'm bigger. There's more of me, so I'm more wet.:

In a very short time all four of them were so drenched there was little point in comparisons. Fortunately, as they crested a rise in the trail, the tanners' holding came into sight on the other side of a small valley. Neither Companion needed urging toward the river running through the valley center although they both stopped well back from the bank. The water was brown and running fast, the log bridge nearly awash.

:What do you think? Is it safe?:

Gervis stepped cautiously out onto the edge of the logs. *:If we move quickly.:*

But Calida hesitated.

:What is it?:

:Calida says the river's already undermining the bridge supports. That the bridge is going to wash away.:

:Tell her that if it does, better we're all on the side with shelter. I'm half drowned and half frozen and Brock's got to be colder still. She's got to get him out of this weather.:

Eyes wide, the mare stepped up beside Gervis, who took her arrival as his cue to leap forward. One stride, two, three. As Jors watched anxiously from the other shore, Calida slowly followed, placing each hoof with care.

Wood screamed a protest as the bridge supports caved.

The huge logs dipped and skewed out from the bank, dragged by the river.

Calida half-reared as her front hooves scrambled for purchase in the mud.

Brock bounced over the cantle and disappeared.

"No!" Jors threw himself to the ground. Stumbling to the Companion's side, he grabbed the mare's saddle and heaved. Step by step, as she managed to work her way forward, he worked his way back until, to his amazement, he saw a very muddy Brock holding on with both hands to Calida's tail, his feet in the river. A heartbeat later, with solid ground beneath all four of them, he dropped to his knees and gathered Brock up into his arms.

"Are you all right?"

He looked more surprised than frightened and returned the hug with wet enthusiasm. "I fell."

"I know. The bridge broke."

Brock twisted around to look and clutched at Jors' arm. "I'm sorry!"

"It's okay. It wasn't your fault." His heart slamming painfully against his ribs, Jors grabbed a stirrup and hauled himself onto his feet. "Come on, we're almost there."

The tanners' holding looked deserted as they stumbled up to the buildings. Jors called out a greeting, but the wind and rain whipped the words out of his mouth.

Brock grabbed his arm. "Smoke," he said, pointing to the thin grey line rising reluctantly from a chimney. "I'm cold."

"Me, too."

All thoughts turned to a warm fire as they made their way over to the building, the Companions crowding in close under the wide eaves.

:We'll be right back as soon as we find someone.:

:Hurry, Chosen.: Gervis sounded completely miserable. Covered in mud almost to his withers, his mane hanging in a tangled, sodden mass, he looked very little like the gleaming creature who'd left the Waystation that morning. Calida, if anything, looked worse.

Jors considered leaving Brock with the Companions, but the other man's breathing sounded unnaturally hoarse, so he beckoned him forward as he tried the door. The sooner he got him inside the better.

The door opened easily. It hadn't even been latched.

"Hello?"

Stepping inside wasn't so much a step into warmth as a step into a space less cold. It looked like they'd found the family's main living quarters, although the room was so dim it was difficult to tell for sure. The only light came from a small fire smouldering on the fieldstone hearth and a tallow lamp on the floor close beside a cradle.

"No." Brock charged across the room, trailing a small river in his wake. "No fire beside baby!"

Remembering what Lorrin had told him about Brock and babies, Jors held his position by the door. The younger of two, what he knew about babies could be inscribed on the head of a pin with room left over for the lyrics to *Kerowyn's Ride.*

Squatting, Brock picked up the lamp. "No fire beside baby," he repeated, began to rise, and paused. "Baby?" Leaning forward, he peered into the cradle.

"Is it all right?" The lamp and the fire together threw barely enough light for Jors to see Brock. He couldn't see the baby at all.

Setting the lamp down again, Brock stretched both hands into the cradle. When he stood and turned, he was holding a limp infant across both palms, his broad features twisted in sorrow. "Baby is dead."

:Jors!:

Jors spun around as the door slammed open and five people surged into the room. They froze for an instant, then the man in front howled out a wordless challenge and charged.

Bending, Jors captured his attacker's momentum, then he straightened, throwing the other man to the floor hard enough to knock him breathless. The immediate threat removed, he faced the remaining two men and two women. "I am Herald Jors. Who is in charge here?"

"I am," the older woman snarled.

The hate in her eyes nearly drove Jors back a step.

He didn't need Brock's whispered "mean lady" to know

who she was. It took an effort, but he kept his voice calm and understanding as he said, "The child was dead when we arrived."

"Dory came to say the babe was sick, not *dead*," she spat as the younger woman ran silently forward and snatched the body from Brock's hands. "The Moonling killed him."

"He did not…"

"You're here, and he's there," she sneered. "You can't see what he did."

Spreading his hands, he added a mild warning to his tone. "And you weren't even in the building. I understand this is a shock…"

"You understand nothing, Herald." She placed a hand on the backs of the two remaining men and shoved. "Have the guts to support your brother!"

They sprang forward, looking like nothing so much as a pair of whipped dogs.

"Jors?"

He ducked an awkward blow. "Outside, Brock. Now!" If anything happened to him, the Companions would get Brock to safety.

"There's two of you and one of him, you idiots! Don't let him protect the half-wit!" *:Chosen?:*

:It's all right.:

Fortunately, neither man was much of a fighter. Jors could have ended it quickly, but as they'd just suffered a sudden terrible loss and weren't thinking clearly, he didn't want to do any serious damage. After a moment, he realized that had it not been for the old woman goading them on, neither would have been fighting. *Maybe I should have Gervis deal with…*

He'd forgotten the first brother. The piece of firewood caught him on the side of the head. As he started to fall, he felt unfriendly hands grab his body.

"No!"

Then the hands were ripped away, and he hit the floor. Two bodies hit the floor after him, closely followed by the third.

"Never hit a Herald!"

"Get up, you cowards! That's a Moonling – not a real man!"

"But, Ma…"

"He killed *my* grandson!"

Hers. Jors thought muzzily. *Not grief. Anger. Anger at the loss of a possession.*

"You never loved him!"

Apparently, the child's mother agreed.

"You always complained about him! You said if he didn't stop crying you were going to strangle him! If anyone killed him…"

"Don't you raise your voice to me, you cow. If you were a better…"

"ENOUGH!"

The doors slammed open again. Hooves clattering against the floorboards, the Companions moved to flank Brock. From Jors' position on the floor, it looked as if there were significantly more than a mere eight muddy white legs.

"Don't lie there with your idiot mouths open! They're just horses!"

"They're not *just* horses, you stupid old woman!"

:Gervis?:

:I'm here, Heartbrother.:

Jors felt better about his chance of recovery. Gervis was angry, but not frantic.

"A baby is dead. Is time for crying, not fighting. A Herald is hurt. You hurt a Herald."

:Is that Brock standing up to the mean lady?:

:It is.:

:Good for him.:

"You will cry, and you will make the Herald better!"

"I will *not.*"

No mistaking that hate-filled voice.

"Then *I* will."

Nor the voice of the child's mother.

For the first time, Brock sounded confused. "You will cry?"

"No. I will help the Herald."

:Out of spite…:

:You need help, Heartbrother. Your head is bleeding. Spiteful help is still help.:

Jors got one arm under him and tried to rise. *:If you say…:*

:Chosen!:

His Companion's cry went with him into darkness.

*

Jors woke to the familiar and comforting smell of a stable. For a moment, he thought he'd dozed off on foal-watch, then he moved and the pain in his head brought everything back. *:Gervis!:*

:I'm here.: A soft nose nuzzled his cheek. *:Just open your eyes.:*

Even moving his eyelids hurt, but he forced them up. Fortunately, the stable was dark, the brightest things in it the two Companions. He could just barely make out Brock tucked up against Calida's side, wrapped in a blanket and nearly buried in straw. *:How long?:*

:From almost dark to just after moonrise. Long enough I was starting to worry.:

He stretched up a hand and stroked the side of Gervis' face. *:Sorry.:*

:The young female made tea for your head. There's a closed pot buried in the straw by your side.:

The tea was still warm and tasted awful, but Gervis made him drink the whole thing. *:I take it we're in the stable because you and Calida wouldn't leave me?:*

:The old woman said the young woman could do as she pleased, but not in her house. I do not want you to be in her house.: The obvious distaste in the young stallion's mental voice was hardly surprising. Even on short acquaintance the old woman was as nasty a piece of work as Jors ever wanted to get close to. *:Brock told two of the young males to carry you here.:*

:He just told them what to do and they did it?:

:They are used to being told what to do.:

:Good point,: Jors acknowledged.

:And,: Gervis continued, *:I think they were frightened when they realized they had struck down a Herald.:*

:They knew *I was a Herald!:*

:Knowing and realizing are often different. Had the blow struck by the child's father been any lower, they would have killed you, and that frightened them, too. They were thankful Brock took charge. He saw you were tended to, he was assured you would live without damage, he groomed us both, and then he cried himself to sleep.:

:Poor guy. Good thing he was there. If he hadn't been, I wouldn't have put it past the mean lady to have finished the job and buried both our bodies.:

:The Circle would know.:

:We'd still be dead. Is this why Calida insisted on bringing him?:

:She has told her Chosen we need no assistance and convinced her not to ride to the rescue. The Herald Isabel agreed, but only because she felt the townspeople would lay the blame on Brock.:

:That's ridiculous.:

Gervis sighed, blowing sweet, hay-scented breath over Jors' face. *:There is already much talk against him taking a Companion.:*

All of which he needed to know, but didn't answer his question. About to ask it again, he stopped short. *:Calida can reach Isabel from here? I couldn't reach you from here!:*

:Nor I you.:

He sounded so put out by it, Jors couldn't prevent a smile. *:Never mind, Heartbrother. Calida and her Chosen have been together for many years; when we've been together for that long, I'll hear you if I'm in Sorrows and you're in Sensholding.:*

:I'd rather we were never that far apart.:

Jors wrapped one hand in Gervis' silken mane. *:Me either.:*

:Sleep now, Chosen. It will be morning soon enough.:

When Jors opened his eyes again, weak autumn sunlight filtered into the stable. An attempt to rise brought Gervis in through the open door. He pulled himself to his feet with a handful of mane, and throwing an arm over his Companion's back, managed to get to where he could relieve himself.

:The old woman made them bury the child this morning.:

:They're only a day's ride from town; they can't wait for a priest?:

:The bridge is gone. The priest cannot come.: He pawed the ground with a front hoof and added. *:I don't think the old woman would send for a priest even if he could come.:*

:Do you know where they are?:

:Yes.:

Jors took a deep breath and, holding it, managed to swing himself up on Gervis' bare back. *:Let's go, then.:*

The tanners had a graveyard in a small clearing cupped by the surrounding oak forest. When Jors arrived, the three men had just finished filling in the tiny hole. As Jors stopped, half hidden by a large sumac, Brock wiped the tears from his face on Calida's mane and stepped up to the grave.

"There is no priest. I will say goodbye to the baby."

"I'm not listening to a half-wit say anything," the old woman snarled. She turned on one heel and started down the hill. "I only came to see the job was done right. Enric, Kern, Simen; back to work, there's hides to be sammied."

Two of the three moved to her side, the third looked toward the young woman and hesitated. "He was my son, Ma."

"He was my son, Ma." She threw it mockingly over her shoulder. "Look around you, Simen. I've buried a son, two daughters, and a husband besides, and it don't make hides tan themselves. Stay and listen to the half-wit if you want."

"Dory?"

She lifted stony eyes to Simen's face. "Better do as your ma says," she sneered. "'Cause you always do as your ma says."

Scarred hands curled into fists, but they stayed at his side. "Fine. I'll go."

"I don't care."

"Fine." But when he turned, Brock was in his way. Jors tensed to urge Gervis forward, but at the last instant, for no clear reason, he changed his mind.

"Stay and say goodbye." A heavy shove rocked him in place, but didn't move him. "Stay." And then gently. "Say goodbye to baby."

Simen stared down into Brock's face, then wordlessly turned back to the grave.

Brock returned to his place and rubbed his nose on his sleeve. "Sometimes," he said, "babies die. Mamas and papas love them, and hug them, and kiss them, and feed them, and they die. Nobody did anything bad. Everyone is sorry. The baby wasn't bad. Babies are good. Goodbye, baby."

"His name," Simen said, so quietly Jors almost missed it, "was Tamas."

Brock nodded solemnly. "Goodbye, Tamas. Everyone is sorry." He lifted his head and stared at Tamas' parents standing hunch-shouldered, carefully apart. "Now, you cry."

Dory shook her head. "Crying is for the weak."

"You have tears." Brock tapped his own chest. "In here. Tears not cried go bad. Bad tears make you hurt."

"You heard Aysa. She buried a son and two daughters. She never cried."

"She is the mean lady," Brock said sadly. "You can't be the mean lady." He opened his arms and, before Dory could move, wrapped her in one of his all-encompassing hugs.

Jors knew from experience that when Brock hugged, he held nothing back.

It was a new experience for Dory.

She blinked twice, drew in a long shuddering breath, then clutched at his tattered sweater and began to sob. After a moment, Brock reached out one hand, grabbed Simen and pulled him into the embrace.

"Cry now," he commanded.

"I…" Simen shook his head and tried to pull away. Brock pulled him closer, pushing Dory into his arms and wrapping himself around them both. Simen stiffened then made a sound, very like his son might have made, and gave himself over to grief. All three of them sank to their knees.

:These people need help.:

Gervis shifted his head. *:It seems they're getting it.:*

With the funeral over, Jors pulled himself into something resembling official shape and sought out Aysa.

"Your son attacked a Herald."

"His son just died. He was mad with grief."

"You goaded his brothers…"

"To stand by him," she sneered triumphantly. "I never told no one to hit you. And now I'm givin' you and that half-wit food and shelter. You can't ask for more, Herald."

Given that he and Brock were trapped on her side of the river, he supposed he'd better not. "About the bridge…"

Without the bridge, there was no way back. The river wasn't particularly wide, but the water ran deep and fast.

"You come out here to stick your nose in on us, then you're stuck out here till we head in to town, and we ain't headin' nowheres until them hides is done. We wasted time enough with Dory having that baby. You want to leave before that, then you and the halfwit can rebuild the bridge yourself."

"That's fair. I can't expect you to drop everything and assist me." His next words wiped the triumphant sneer from her face. "I'll have them send a crew out from town."

"You can't get word to town."

He smiled, hoping he looked a lot more confident of the conversation's outcome than he felt. "There's a Herald there, and I already have. By this time tomorrow, there'll be a dozen people in the valley."

"Liar."

"Heralds can't lie, Ma."

"Shut up!" Aysa half turned, and Kern winced away as though he expected to be hit. Lip curled, she turned back to Jors. "I don't want a dozen people in the valley! And it don't take a dozen people anyway. And the water won't be down enough tomorrow."

"Then I'll have them come when the water goes down."

"You won't have no one come. My boys'll rebuild."

"Then the townspeople can help."

"My boys don't need help. They ain't got brains for much, but they can do that. You let them know in town I'm hostin' you *and* the half-wit till then."

It was a grudgingly offered truce, but he'd take it. Jors wasn't surprised that Aysa'd refused help. The last thing she'd want would be her sons exposed to more people, to people who'd make them realize they were entitled to be treated with kindness. Over the next few days, while they waited for the water to recede, she proved that by keeping him by her side, keeping him from interacting with anyone else at the holding.

Brock, she considered no threat. Which was a mistake.

Because Brock treated everyone with kindness.

"You call that supple? I could do better chewin' it! How could you be doin' this all your life and still be no damned good? You're pathetic." Enric and Kern leaped back as she threw the piece of finished leather down at their feet. "Pathetic," she repeated and stomped away.

"Mean lady calls me names, too," Brock sighed, coming out from behind the fleshing beam and picking up the hide.

Enric ripped it out of his hands. "We ain't half-wits."

"Mean lady calls me half-wit. Not you."

"You *are* a half-wit!"

"Are you pathetic?"

Kern jerked forward, face flushed. "You callin' us pathetic?"

"No. It hurts when people call names." Brock looked from one to the other. "Doesn't it hurt?"

"If your half-wit falls in a liming pit," Aysa snarled as Jors caught up, "my boys'll stand there and laugh."

"You taught them that."

"I'm all they got."

"They're terrified of you."

"Good."

"Dory isn't."

"You think one of my boys is stupid enough to pick up a weakling?" Aysa nodded toward the garden where Dory heaped cabbage into a basket. "But she does what I say like the rest. If she doesn't like it, she can leave any time."

While they watched, Dory lifted the basket, gave a little cry and let it fall.

Aysa snorted. "'Course that baby left her stupidly weak."

Jors took a step toward the garden, but stopped as Simen came out of the chicken house and hurried across to his wife.

"Simen! You get back to work, you lazy pig."

His mother's voice froze him in his tracks. Then he shook himself and began retrieving the spilled cabbages.

"Simen!"

He ignored her.

"This is your fault, Herald. Turning a woman's family against her." Muttering under her breath, she strode toward them.

Dory looked up, saw her coming and stood, hands on hips.

"You think you can face me down, girl? Simen, get up!"

He stood.

"Now get back to work."

He took a step forward and put his hands on Dory's shoulders. "When I'm finished here, Ma."

Aysa's mouth worked for a moment, but no sound emerged. Finally, she spun on one heel and stomped away.

The comer of Simen's mouth curled. "You'd best help here, Herald. I wouldn't follow her right now."

*

The river was low enough the next day.

The bridge took only a day longer to rebuild, and for the most part, involved fitting the original pieces back into place.

Jors stared at the completed bridge in amazement. "That's incredible."

"Nothin' incredible about it, Herald," Enric snorted. "Damned thing goes out every other season. Easier to build it so it breaks apart clean."

His bare torso red with cold, Kern shrugged into a sheepskin coat. "Supports slip out so they don't shatter, logs end up in the same place, we float 'em back and rebuild. Any idiot can do it."

"Trust me, I've crossed a hundred rivers – or maybe a couple of rivers a hundred times – but I've never seen anything like this."

"Ma says it's not..." Simen paused, frowned, and looked up at the Herald. "It's really good?"

"It's really good."

The brothers exchanged confused looks, and Jors had the horrible suspicion this was the first time they'd ever been praised for anything.

*

The next day, while Jors was checking Calida's girth strap for the trip back to town, Dory came out of the house with a bundle. "It's for Brock," she said, folding back a corner. "I want you to give it to him for me."

At first Jors thought it was white leather. Made sense; they were tanners after all. Then he realized the leather had been cut and sewn into a fair approximation of Herald's Whites. Dory had clearly taken the pattern from his and sized it to fit Brock.

"I saw he didn't have none of his own."

Oh, help. "Dory, you know he's not… "

"Brother Herald! We go now? What you got?" His hands and Dory's together closed the bundle.

"It's a surprise," Dory said, her cheeks crimson. "For later."

"Not for now?"

"No."

"Okay." He took Calida's reins and stood, waiting patiently while Jors tied the bundle behind Gervis' saddle.

:You seem upset, Chosen.:

:I can't tell her Brock's not an actual Herald while he's standing there. He'll say he is, I'll say he isn't, and I'm not sure that in this place, at this time, I'd win the argument.:

:You shouldn't argue.:

:Oh, that's helpful.:

:Thank you.:

The whole family went with them to the bridge. Jors didn't know why the rest came, but he was certain Aysa just wanted to make sure they were off her land. He wanted to say something, something that would convince them they didn't have to live inside the darkness of an old woman's anger, but before he could think of the right words, Brock hugged Dory. And Simen. And Enric. And Kern.

Then he scrambled up into the saddle and, from the safety of Calida's back, took a deep breath, looked Aysa in the eye, and spoke directly to her for the first time. "Why don't you love your babies?"

Her lip curled. "I buried my babies, half-wit."

He nodded toward the three young men standing to her right. "Not them."

She turned, looked at her sons, looked back at Brock and muttered, "Half-wit." But there was little force behind it.

Jors had no idea he was going to do what he did until he did it.

*

"Jors, you hugged mean lady."

"Yeah. I know." Although he still couldn't believe it. "Everyone else got hugged, I just…"

She'd pushed him away with such force that he'd slammed back into Gervis' shoulder.

"You are the bravest Herald. Ever, ever."

"Thank you."

Then she'd snarled something incomprehensible, turned, and stomped away.

He'd probably accomplished nothing at all by it. The bundle Dory had given him pushed against the small of his back.

*

The weather remained clear and cool, and just as the sun was setting, they stopped outside the village.

"Gate will close when sun is set," Brock warned.

"I know. Brock, I think you should go back to Haven with Isabel."

"Lots of Heralds in Haven?"

"Yes."

Brock sighed and shook his head. "No. I have to stay here. I am the only Herald."

"Brock, you're not..." He couldn't say it. Brock waited patiently for a moment then smiled.

"Is it later?"

"Yes."

"What's Dory's surprise?"

"Uh... it's uh..."

Both Companions turned their heads to look at him. Their expressions said, *this is up to you.*

:He believes he is a Herald.:

:Yes, but...:

:And he acts accordingly.:

*

"I couldn't do it, Isabel. They're just clothes. and I know that, but if I gave Brock those Whites, then there'd be fake Heralds showing up all over the place."

"A bad precedent to be sure," the older Herald agreed.

"There has to be a line, and that line has to be the Companions. Sometimes it seems like we're barely keeping order in chaos now. I couldn't... No matter how much..." Jors ran both hands back through his hair. He couldn't believe how much the decision, the right decision had felt like betrayal. "It wouldn't make any difference to Brock. He knows who and what he is, but for the others in the village, those who made fun and called him names..."

"Come here, I want to show you something." Isabel took his arm and pulled him to the window. "What do you see?"

Jors squinted down into the stable yard. "Brock's grooming Gervis again."

"While you four were gone, I talked to a lot of people. Seems that whenever a Herald comes into this village, the Companion manages to spend time with Brock. Even if it's only a moment or two." They watched as Calida crossed the yard and tried to shoulder Gervis away. Brock laughed and told her to wait her turn. "You were right not to give him the Whites," Isabel continued, "but you were also right when you said it makes no difference. He couldn't be Chosen because, as Heralds, we have to face dangers he'd never understand, but the Companions know him. All Brock needs from us is our love and support. Now, since Healer Lorrin has finally allowed me out of bed, what do you say you and I go down there and give our brother a hand with the four-foots?"

Jors grinned as Brock gamely tried to brush both tails at once.

Heralds wear shiny white.

Brock wore his Whites on the inside.

ALL THE AGES OF MAN

I'm too young for this."

Although Jors had spoken the words aloud, thrown them, as it were, out onto the wind without expecting an answer, he received one anyway.

:So you keep saying.:

"Doesn't make it any less true." He was alone – although he wouldn't be soon – he could hold an apparently one-sided conversation if he wanted to.

:You are experienced in riding circuit,: his Companion reminded him. *:All you must do is teach what you know.:*

Jors snorted and shifted in the saddle. "So *you* keep saying."

Gervis snorted in turn. *:Then perhaps you should listen.:*

"I'm not a teacher."

:You are a Herald. More importantly, you are needed.:

And that was why they were heading north-east, out to the edge of their sector to meet with Herald Jennet and her greenie. The courier who'd brought the news of Jennet's mother's sickness and recall to Haven, had also brought the news to Jors that he'd been assigned as Jennet's replacement and would be finishing out the last eleven months of the greenie's internship.

The greenie's name was Alyise, her Companion's name was Donnel, and that was pretty much all Jors knew. He couldn't remember ever seeing anyone of that name amidst the Greys during the rare times he'd been at the Collegium over the last few years, and he only remembered her Companion as a long-legged colt.

The thing was, he liked being on the road, and he much preferred the open spaces of the Borders to any city, so he went back on Circuit as fast as he could be reassigned. That didn't give him much time to learn about the latest Chosen, and when he did meet up with other Heralds, he was much more interested in finding out what his year-mates had been doing.

"Jennet has to be ten years older than I am. At least. And she's a woman."

Strands of the Companion's mane slid across Jors' fingers like white silk as Gervis tossed his head. *:What does her being a woman have to do with this?:*

"Women are better at teaching girls. They understand girls. Me…" He rubbed a dribble of sweat off the back of his neck. "…I don't get girls at all."

:You seemed to understand Herald Erica. I remember her continuously agreeing with you.:

"Continuously agreeing? What are you talking about?"

:Raya and I could hear her quite clearly outside the Waystation. She kept yelling yes. Yes! Yes! Yes!:

"Oh, ha ha. Very funny." Jors could feel Gervis' amusement – the young stallion did indeed think it was very funny. "As I recall, Erica and I weren't the only two keeping company that night."

:We were quiet.:

"Well, I'm sorry we kept you from your beauty sleep, and you needn't worry about it happening again for, oh, about eleven months."

:You do not know that the new Herald will find you distasteful. Raya told me that her Herald found you pleasant.:

Jors sighed. Pleasant. Well, he supposed it was preferable to the alternative. "Thank you. But that's not the point. I'll be Alyise's teacher, her mentor; I can't take advantage of my position of power."

:You will be Heralds together.:

"Yes, but…" He felt a subtle shift of smooth muscles below him echoed by a definite shift of attention, and fell silent.

:Inar says we will meet in time for us to return to the Waystation outside of Appleby before full dark.:

If that was true, and Jors had no reason to doubt Jennet's Companion, they were a lot closer to the crossroad than he'd thought. He glanced over his shoulder to check on Bucky and found the pack-mule tucked up close where Gervis' tail could keep the late summer insects off his face. And that was another possible problem. Mules were mules regardless of who they worked for, and mules that worked for Heralds could be just as obstinate and hard to get along with as any other. They'd be adding a new mule to the mix.

It was a good thing Companions always got along.

And speaking of…

"Why didn't Donnel contact you? Can't he reach this far?"

:Inar is senior to Donnel, as you will be senior to his Chosen.:

"You'll be senior to Donnel, as well then."

:Yes.: Sleek white sides rose and fell as Gervis sighed.

Jors grinned. "Wishing Alyise's Companion was a mare?"

His grin broadened as it became quite clear that Gervis had no intention of answering.

*

"She's a good kid," Jennet said, glancing over at where the youngest of the three Heralds carefully packed away the remains of the meal they'd shared. "Eager, enthusiastic…"

"Exhausting?" Jors suggested as her voice trailed off.

"A little," the older Herald admitted with a smile. "But you're a lot younger than I am, you should be able to keep up."

"That's just it. I'm too young to be doing this. I'm no teacher."

"You have doubts."

He only just managed not to roll his eyes. "Well, yes."

"Does your Companion doubt you?"

"Gervis?" Jors turned in time to see Gervis rising to his feet after what had clearly been a vigorous roll, his gleaming white coat flecked with bits of grass. "Gervis has never doubted me."

"Then, if you can't believe in yourself, believe in your Companion. And now that I've gifted you with my aged wisdom…" Grinning, she bent and lifted her saddle. "…we'd best get back on the road."

Lifting his own saddle, Jors fell into step beside her. "I'm sorry to hear about your mother."

"Yes, well, she wasn't young when I was born, and she's never been what you could call strong, so I can't say that I'm surprised. I'm just glad that the Borders are so quiet right now and that there was someone close enough." She smiled so gratefully at him that Jors felt himself flush.

*

Inar, given his head, had disappeared southward almost too fast for the eye to follow. One moment he and his Herald were a white blur against the gold of summer-dried gasses, and the next, they were gone.

Gone. Leaving Jors alone with Alyise.

Alone with an attractive nineteen-year-old girl.

No. Alone with another Herald.

One he just happened to be responsible for.

The four years between them felt more like four months.

I'm too young…

:She's a Herald. That makes her responsible for herself.:

:I was broadcasting?:

Gervis snorted. *:Donnel probably heard you.:*

Jors doubted that since Donnel – with a fair bit of that long-legged colt in him still – was dancing sideways away from a bobbing yellow wildflower. Alyise was laughing, probably at something Donnel had said. Their mule, right out at the end of the lead rope, turned his head just far enough for Jors to see that he looked resigned about the whole thing.

Which reminded Jors of something he'd meant to ask Jennet and forgotten. No matter. Alyise would know what had happened to their second mule.

"Spike?" She giggled. "Oh, Jennet left him back at the Waystation Supply post saying you'd have enough on your plate without having to deal with Spike too. He's not a pleasant fellow, although, honestly, I think most of it's an act and he's really much nicer than he pretends. You know?"

Jors had no time to answer. He suspected she hadn't intended him to as she rattled on without pausing.

"She left a lot of her gear there, except for the bits she gave to me. I seem to go through soap really, really quickly, I can't think why, I mean, we're all in Whites, but if there's something to smudge on, I'll smudge. I may be the only Herald ever who really appreciated her Greys. So Jennet gave me her extra soap, and a tunic that was getting too tight for her – across the shoulders of course, not in front, because I'm well, a little better endowed there – but no worry about her being caught short, because she didn't leave behind or give me anything she'll need because she's heading home. But you knew that didn't you, because you were there when she left."

The punctuating smile was dazzling.

*

The Waystation outside Appleby was much like every other Waystation; there was a corral for the mules, a snug lean-to for the Companions, a good-sized, well-stocked storeroom, and a single room for the Heralds. The biggest difference was that the fireplace had been filled in with a small box-stove, flat-topped for cooking and considerably more efficient at heating the space.

"Not to mention there'll be a lot less warm air sucked up the chimney," Jors observed, examining the stove-pipes. This was new since the last time he'd been by.

"I think it's less romantic, though."

"What?"

Alyise smiled as he turned. "I think a stove is less romantic than an open fire. Don't you think there's just something so sensual about the dancing flames and the flickering golden light?"

"Light." Jors cleared his throat and tried again. "We'd better light the lanterns."

She pushed russet curls back off her face with one hand, grey eyes gleaming in the dusk. "Or instead of lighting the lanterns, we could just leave the doors of the stove open and sit together close to the fire."

"Fire."

"Pardon?"

"You light the fire." His palms were sweaty. "In the stove," he expanded as she stared at him, head cocked. "So we can cook. I have to go check on Gervis."

:I'm fine.:

:Good.: He got outside to find his Companion standing by the door and gazing at him with some concern. *:She's... I mean, I'm supposed to be teaching her.:*

:Donnel says his Chosen is glad you are an attractive young man. She's been with Jennet for seven months and had little opportunity to share her bed.:

:Hey, I've been on my own for eight, and I've...: He paused as Gervis snorted. *:Yeah. Sorry. Way too much information. The point is, it wouldn't be right.:*

:If that's how you feel.:

:It is.:

:Good luck.:

:Oh, that's very helpful.:

:Thank you.:

"Never let anyone tell you that Companions can't be as sarcas-

tic as cats," Jors muttered to himself as he turned and went back inside. The curve of Alyise's bare back stopped him cold. Her pants hung low on the flare of her hips, low enough to expose the dimples just below her waist.

She smiled at him over her shoulder as she pulled a long, sleeveless tunic out of her pack. "I just had to get into something that wasn't all sweaty. I don't know what it is about spending the day in the saddle that makes me so damp since Donnel's doing most of the work, but from my breast bands right on out everything is just soaked through. I guess the good news is that, at this time of the year, I can rinse them out tonight and they'll be dry by morning, unless it rains, of course, but I don't think it's going to. There's really no point in having the village laundry deal with them." Her brow wrinkled as she pushed her head through the tunic's wide neck. "Does this village even have a laundry?"

"Laundry?" He tried not to stare at the pale swell of her breasts as she pulled the tunic down, and turned to light one of the lamps with shaking hands. He was not ready for this kind of responsibility.

"Men."

Was she allowed to laugh at him? There was too much about this mentoring that he didn't know.

"I don't suppose you even noticed," she continued, slipping out of her pants. "Ah, that's better. Shall you cook or shall I?"

"Me!" Cooking would be a welcome distraction. "You can tell me about your time with Jennet. So I know what you've covered… done."

"Okay; how much of…"

"Everything!"

Everything took them through dinner and into bed. Separate beds. Alyise seemed fine with that, Jors noticed thankfully, since he wasn't certain his resolve would stand up against a determined assault. Long after her breathing had evened out into the long rhythms of sleep, he lay staring up at the rough wood of the ceiling and wondered just how authoritarian he was supposed to be. All Heralds were equals, that was a given. Except when they weren't, and that was tacitly understood. *I'm just not ready for this yet.*

:Sleep now, Heartbrother.: Gervis's mental touch was gentle. *:Many tasks seem less daunting in the morning.:*

*

Jors woke just after sunrise to discover that Alyise had already gone out to feed and water the mules.

"I can never stay in bed after I wake up," she explained with a sunny smile. "My mother used to say it's because I was afraid I'd miss something, but I think it's because I didn't want to get bounced on by my younger sisters, and I'll tell you, that habit stood me in good stead when I was a Grey, because you know how hard it is to get going some mornings, and the first up has the first shot at the hot water and there were mostly girls in my year; six of us and one boy. What about yours?"

"My?" When did she breathe?

"Your year; how many boys and girls in your year?"

"Oh. Three boys, two girls."

"How… nice."

He heard Donnel snort, realized she was staring at him, and a moment later realized why. He'd gotten a little panicked when he'd seen her bed was empty and raced outside wearing only the light cotton drawstring pants he'd slept in. With the early morning sun behind him, he might as well be naked. :*Oh, yeah. This is going to help me maintain some kind of authority.*:

:*Authority does not come from your clothing.*:

And that would have been more reassuring had his Companion not sounded like he found the entire situation entirely too funny. :*Maybe not, but it sure doesn't come from…*: It occurred to him that while he was standing talking to Gervis, Alyise was still staring. Smiling appreciatively. "I'll just go and get dressed. We'll be heading into Appleby right after we eat."

And thank any Gods who may be listening for that, he thought as he made as dignified a retreat as possible into the Waystation.

*

Appleby wasn't so much a village as it was a market and clearing center for the surrounding orchards that gave it its name. Jors told the younger Herald all he knew about both the area and the inhabitants as they rode in from the Waystation, but since his available information ran out some distance before they arrived, Alyise took over the conversation.

Her mother made a terrific apple dumpling, but wouldn't give out the recipe no matter how much Alyise or her sisters begged.

Donnel was very fond of apples, especially the small, sweet, pink ones that grew further north.

She loved apples sliced and dried, and hoped she'd be able to buy some of last years if they had a moment before they left town.

Her grandfather used to carve apples and dry them whole

and they turned into the most cunning old men and old women dolls' heads.

Just when Jors was about to suggest she stop talking, she finished her story about how an apple peel taken off in one unbroken spiral would give the initial of one's true love when tossed over a shoulder and fell silent, straightening in the saddle and transforming from girl to Herald.

:Neat trick.:

:Why does she need to be anything but what she is when she is with you?: Gervis asked reasonably.

:She doesn't.:

:And why do you…:

:Because I'm her teacher!:

:Herald Jennet was also her teacher. Do you think Herald Jennet behaved differently than herself?:

:Herald Jennet has had more time to be herself!: Jors pointed out.

Gervis tossed his head, setting his bridle bells ringing as they passed the first of the buildings. *:You are not Herald Jennet,:* he said as the first wave of laughing children broke around them.

:That's what I keep saying!:

The Companion carefully sidestepped an overly adventurous and remarkably grubby little boy. *:Maybe you should try listening.:*

And that was all he was willing to say.

"Go not to your Companion for advice," Jors muttered under his breath. *"For they will tell you to figure it out for yourself."*

*

Judgments in Appleby were, not surprisingly, mostly

about apples. More surprisingly, Jors found Alyise to be an attentive listener – both to the petitioners and to him. Although she deferred to Jors as the senior Herald, she expressed her opinions clearly and concisely when asked for them and, in turn, asked intelligent questions when she needed more information. Having been more than a little afraid of what the day would bring, Jors was impressed and grateful that he could set aside personal doubts and concentrate on the job at hand.

Late that afternoon, when they'd finished with official business and had moved on to the more social aspects of being a Herald – trading the gossip that kept the far-flung corners of the kingdom telling the same stories – Jors glanced over at Alyise within a circle of teenage girls and wondered if it counted as a conversation when everyone seemed to be talking at once.

"Herald Jors."

He turned to see the eldest of the village councilors holding out a cup of cider.

"Don't worry, it's one of this year's first pressings. Windfall from the early apples. It has absolutely no trade value, so you needn't fear you're being bribed."

A tentative sip curled his tongue. "Tart," he gasped.

"A little young," the councillor admitted, grinning. "And if you don't mind my saying, you seem a little young yourself to be teaching the ray of sunshine there."

"I've been doing this for a while, Councillor." On the outside, Jors remained calm and confident. Inside, a little voice was saying, *Oh, that's just great. It's obvious to everyone.* "And Alyise is a trained Herald. I'm only here to help guide her through her first Circuit.

"Oh, I'm not criticizing, lad. And given that one's energy, it's probably best you're no greybeard. I imagine she'd be the death of an older man."

The councillor obviously believed he was sleeping with Alyise. That was a belief he'd have to nip in the bud. "Heralds aren't in the habit of taking advantage of their Interns."

"Advantage?" The elderly councillor glanced over at Alyise and began to laugh so hard he passed a mouthful of cider out his nose. "Oh, lad," he gasped when he had breath enough to speak again. "You *are* young."

There wasn't a lot Jors could say to that.

*

:You seem fine in the villages,: Gervis pointed out as they headed toward the Border.

:It's different in the villages.: Jors told him. *:We have well-defined roles, and I know what I'm supposed to do.:*

:You've always known what to do in a Waystation before. You've always known what to do with another Herald before.:

He glanced over at Alyise, who'd turned to check on the mules. *:I've never been responsible for another Herald before.:*

His Companion sighed and raised his head so Jors could get at an elusive itch under the edge of his mane. *:You're beginning to worry me.:*

There wasn't a lot Jors could say to that either.

*

Six days later Alyise handed him a mug of tea and said, "Is it because you like boys? It's just that I've been as obvious as I know how without coming right out and saying we should bed down together," she explained a few moments later, after they'd cleaned up the mess. "I mean, I was with Jennet for seven whole months, and you're cute, and well, it's been a while, you know."

He knew.

"Your ears are very red," she added. "So why don't you want to?"

"It's not that I don't *want* to..." Jors held up a hand and attempted to explain about being responsible and not taking advantage of her while he was in at least a nominal position of power. Alyise didn't seem to quite understand his point.

"I'm fully capable of making my own decisions, and you're a little young to take such a grandfatherly attitude, don't you think?"

"That's it exactly."

She wrinkled her nose, confused. "What's it?"

She was adorable when she wrinkled her nose, and some of the tea had splashed on her tunic drawing his eye right to...

"Maybe you should talk to Donnel about it," he choked out. "I need to check the um... mules."

"I just checked them."

"I meant the... um, stores!"

*

"Gervis explained to Donnel, who explained to me, and I think I understand the problem." Alyise smiled at Jors reassuringly when he came back inside. "I was kind of dumped on you unexpectedly, wasn't I? I mean, there you were, out riding your Circuit, just the two of you, hearing petitions and riding to the rescue and being guys together, and all of a sudden Jennet finds out her mother is sick and you've got me. I know Heralds are supposed to be adaptable and all, but this is a situation that could take some getting used to for you, so I expect it's all a matter of timing."

"Good. So we're, um…" He tried, not entirely successfully, to pull her actual meaning from the cheerful flow of words.

Her smile broadened. "We're good."

"Okay." Still, something felt not quite right. *:Gervis?:*

He could almost see his Companion roll sapphire eyes. *:I dealt with it, Chosen.:*

:But…:

:Let it go.:

Not so much advice as an unarguable instruction.

"So…" Jors brought his attention back to the younger Herald. "…there were some tax problems in the area we're heading for next. We should go over them in case they come up again."

"Jennet and I ran into a few problems just like this, back last month. Well, not just like this because that's one thing I've learned since I've been out is that no two problems are exactly the same no matter how much they seem to be, and…"

He let her words wash over him as he pulled the papers from his pack. So they were good. That was…

…good.

Why did he feel like he was waiting for the other shoe to drop?

*

Last year's tax problems didn't reoccur, but new problems arose, and Jors did his best to guide Alyise through them. She was better with people than he was, and as summer passed into fall, he allowed her to hear those petitions that dealt with social problems and tried to learn from her natural charm as she learned from his experience.

Given her unflagging energy and exuberance, he felt as though he was running full-out to stay ahead of her, and he never felt younger or more unsuited for his position as her teacher as when he saw her in the midst of a crowd of admiring young men.

Not that she ever forgot she was a Herald on duty, it was just…

:Just what, Chosen?:

:You're laughing at me again, aren't you?:

No answer in words, just a strong feeling of amusement. Which was, of course, all the answer Jors needed.

*

Frost had touched the grass by the time they reached the tiny village of Halfrest, grown up not quite a generation before around a campsite that marked the halfway point on a shortcut between two larger towns. A shortcut only because the actual trade road followed the kind of ground sensible people built roads on, rather than taking the direct route more suitable to goats.

Jors had a feeling that without the mule tied to her saddle, Alyise and Donnel would have been bounding like those goats from rock to rock, Alyise chattering cheerfully the entire time as they skirted the edges of crumbling cliffs.

The Waystation was brand new, the wood still pale and raw looking. No corral had been built for the mules, but a rope strung between two trees would take the lead lines, giving them plenty of room to graze. While there was no well, the pond looked crystal clear and cold.

"If you have a Waystation," Jors said as they carried their packs inside, "you're more than just a group of people trying to carve out an uncertain life. You're a real village."

"And that's important to them, to be seen as a real village?"

"This was wilderness when the elders of this village came here with their parents. They're proud of what they've accomplished."

He reminded her of that again as they rode into Halfrest, which was, in point of fact, nothing much more than a group of people trying to carve out an uncertain life. Livestock still shared many of the same buildings as their owners, and function ruled over form. Only the Meeting Hall bore any decoration – graceful, joyful carvings tucked up under the gabled eaves gave some promise of what could be when the townspeople finally got a bit ahead.

"Because a real village has a Meeting Hall?" Alyise asked quietly as they dismounted.

He nodded, and turned to greet the approaching men and women.

They hadn't had an easy year of it. There had been sickness and raiders and heavy rains then sickness again.

"We had no Harvest Festival this year," a weary woman told them, pushing greying hair off her face with a thin hand. "With so many sick, there were few to bring the harvest in, so when the fields were finally clear the time was past. We had little heart for it besides. But there are two pigs fattening, pledged for the festival last spring. One came from my good black sow, and I feel I should be able to slaughter him for my own use."

"He was pledged to the village," an equally weary looking man interrupted.

"He was pledged to the festival!"

As there had been no festival, it would seem sensible to give the pig back to the woman who had pledged it, perhaps requiring her to give some of the meat to those in need.

But this was Alyise's judgment, and Jors sat quietly behind her, allowing her to make up her own mind with no interference from him. He glanced around the Hall, from the work-roughened and exhausted villagers to the sullen knot of teenagers clumped together by the door. No one looked hungry or ill-used, just tired. They'd been working non-stop for weeks. It was no wonder they'd skipped their festival; all they probably wanted was a chance to rest.

"I have heard all sides of the argument," Alyise said at last. "And this is my judgement." She paused, just for a moment, and Jors had the strangest feeling the other shoe was finally dropping. "The pig was pledged to the Harvest Festival. Have the festival."

"But the harvest has been in long since, and…"

"The harvest is in," Alyise interrupted, her smile lighting all the dark corners of the room. "I think that's worth celebrating." Before anyone could protest, she locked eyes with the woman who owned the pig. "Don't you?"

"Well, yes, but…"

"The sickness is past. The raiders have been defeated. And that's worth celebrating, too." The man who had protested the reclaiming of the pig seemed stunned by her smile. "Don't you think so?"

"I guess…"

"And the rains have stopped." She spread her arms and turned to the teenagers by the door. "The sun is shining. Why not celebrate that?"

Shoulders straightened. Tentative smiles answered her question.

No one stood against Alyise's enthusiasm for long. Soon, to Jors' surprise, no one wanted to. The pigs were slaughtered and dressed and put in pits to roast. Tables were set up in the hall. Food and drink began to appear. Musicians brought out their instruments.

"I'd have thought they were too tired to party," Jors murmured as half a dozen girls ran giggling by with armloads of the last bright leaves of fall.

"My mother has a saying; if you don't celebrate your victories, all you remember are your defeats. The food they're eating now won't be enough to make a real difference if the winter is especially hard, but the memories they make, good memories of laughter and fellowship, that could be enough to see them through." Alyise gestured toward the carvings. "They know joy. I just helped them remember they knew. You know?"

He did, actually.

*

:Careful, Chosen.: Gervis adjusted his gait as Jors listed slightly to the left.

"You lied to me." Alyise's Whites were a beacon in the darkness. Which was good, because he didn't think he could find her otherwise. Except that she was on Donnel and that made it pretty obvious where she was, now he considered it.

"What did I lie about?"

"You said that was apple… apple juice."

She giggled. "It was, once."

"Jack. That was apples jack. Apple jack." He wasn't drunk. Heralds did not get drunk on duty, even at impromptu Harvest Festivals where the apple juice wasn't. Which he wouldn't have had any of had Alyise not handed him a huge mug just before they left, to toast the celebration and the celebrants.

Now, the stars spun gently around him, and he suspected

that getting the Companions settled for the night would be interesting.

Fortunately, it seemed that Alyise was less affected.

"Hey." He set his saddle down with exaggerated care. "You had some of that too!"

"Some," she agreed, the dimples appearing. "But I didn't drink it as quickly."

"We were leaving."

"I know. Come on inside."

Her hand was warm on his arm. Then it was warm under his tunic. And her mouth tasted warm and sweet. And… Wait a minute. The sudden surge of desire had chased the last of the apple jack muzziness from his head, and he pulled back. His hands, seemingly with a mind of their own, continued working on her laces. It took an effort, but he managed to still them. "I don't think…"

"What?" She licked her lower lip, the lip he'd just licked.

He couldn't remember what he'd been about to say. *:Gervis?:*

:She's hoping your body's reaction will shove your ridiculous objections aside.:

:What?:

:It was Donnel's suggestion, but it seemed sound. You have made this more complicated than it needs to be, so we have simplified it for you.:

:You got me drunk?:

:Are you drunk?"

:I'm…: He considered for a moment. *:No.:*

:Good. Then no one is being taken advantage of.:

The bunk hit the back of his legs, and he was suddenly lying down holding a soft, willing, body.

:Help.:

His Companion's mental voice held layers of laughter. *:She will stop if you tell her no, Heartbrother.:*

:I don't want to tell her no!:

:We are all aware of that, Chosen. If you don't want to tell her no, then tell her yes.:

Alyise was willing, and he was willing, and while the apple jack had relaxed him, he was still fully rational. Alyise was an adult, and he was an adult. And the Companions believed he wasn't taking advantage of her.

Jors stared up into smiling eyes, and wanted. "Yes," he said.

And that was the last coherent statement he made for a while.

*

Jors stood staring down at the pond, watching the early morning sun tease tendrils of fog off the icy-looking water, trying to work the kinks out of muscles he hadn't used for far too long. Alyise was as enthusiastic in bed as she was about everything else, and he'd been hard pressed to keep up.

He guessed he had been a bit of an ass about that whole position of power thing. Still…

:What is it, Chosen?: Gervis velvet nose prodded him in the back.

:I'm still her mentor for another seven months. What if this changes things between us?:

:You think she will no longer trust your judgement because you have shared her bed?:

Put that way, it sounded a bit insulting. *:Well, no.:*

:Then what is the problem?:

There didn't seem to be one. Jors leaned against his Companion's comforting bulk and thought about it.

He wasn't Jennet.

Alyise was a Herald. That made her responsible for herself.

Donnel said his Chosen was glad he was a young man.

They had well defined roles in the villages.

There was no reason for them not to continue sharing a bed as long as they both remained willing. No reason at all for it to detract from his ability to teach what he knew or learn what she offered.

Jors grinned. He had other nights like last night to look forward to, days of cheerful conversations combined with an enthusiastic welcome to whatever the road ahead might bring, and a high-energy approach to life that definitely got results, since a village-wide party solved a petition about a disputed pig.

His grin faded as a muscle twinged in his back.

"Havens," he sighed as he realized what the next few months would bring, "I'm too old for this."

Gervis weight was suddenly no longer a comforting presence at his back, but rather a short, sharp shove.

The water in the pond was as cold as it looked.

LIVE ON

"Are you the young man who wrote that report about Appleby?"

Heralds didn't tend to grow old. Even in times of peace, they lived lives that lowered the odds of them dying in bed to slightly less than negligible. It seemed that the elderly Herald who'd appeared at Jor's side was the exception to prove the rule. His shoulders were hunched forward, his eyes were red rimmed and moist, he stood with his weight supported on a polished cane, and above the scarf he wore in spite of the heat of a sunny, late spring day, age had pleated his face into a hundred wrinkles.

"Are you deaf, boy? I said, are you the young man who wrote that report about Appleby! Are you Herald Jors?"

Age had roughed his voice but not lessened his volume.

People were beginning to gather, and Jors could see a trio of Companions heading across the field to see what all the noise was about. "I am. I'm Jors."

"Who taught you to write reports? Never mind. You leave too much out. That report about Appleby? All apples."

"That's pretty much all there is in Appleby."

"What? There's no people? No dogs? No cats? No buildings? No apple trees, for pity's sake?"

"Of course there are, and…"

"Of course there are," the elderly Herald snorted. "Why didn't you mention them, then, eh? You mentioned the apples, why not the apple trees?"

Jors smiled and spread his hands. "They didn't do much."

The rheumy eyes narrowed. "Don't get smart with me, boy. I've had my Whites longer than your father's been alive, maybe even your father's father, and there has been a distinct disintegration, no, dispersing, no, *erosion* of writing ability over the last few years." He shook a swollen finger at Jors – or perhaps he merely pointed and it shook on its own, it was hard to tell. "Reports used to say things. Give details. Tell stories. They used to bring Valdemar to life. Now it's all apples!"

Since the older man seemed to be waiting for him to respond, Jors ventured a reasonably sincere, "I'm sorry."

"Don't be sorry. Do it right the next time. Honestly," he muttered, turning and making his way toward the stables. "What are they teaching them when they're in their Greys?"

Jors watched him go, watched him correcting a lateral drift every six steps or so, and wondered if he should have offered his arm.

"I see you've met Herald Tamis."

He turned to see Erica, one of his yearmates, leaning on

the fence, one arm stretched out over the top rail so she could scratch up under Raya, her Companion's mane. "He doesn't like the way I write reports."

"As near as I can tell, he doesn't like the way anyone writes reports." She put a quaver into her voice. "It's all business now, I tell you. No stories." Then her expression changed. "Raya says we shouldn't mock him."

"I wasn't."

She smacked his shoulder with her free hand. "You would have."

"Who is he?" Jors asked, climbing up onto the top rail so he could pay a similar attention to his own Companion. Who seemed to be sulking.

:I was not sulking,: Gervis protested, pushing against Jors' leg almost hard enough to knock him off the fence. *:You were ignoring me.:*

:I wasn't.:

:I had an itch.:

Jors rolled his eyes as he pushed a hand up under the silken mane and began to scratch. *:Better?:*

:Yes.:

"Tamis is a historian," Erica told him. "He has rooms in behind the library – I think they used to be storerooms until he took them over. He's working on the history of the Heralds."

"Why have I never met him?"

"Because you're never here."

Gervis snorted. *:She's right.:*

:I don't like cities. Circuits have to be ridden. I might as well ride them.:

:We.:

:We,: he repeated apologetically. And then something occurred to him. "Don't histories usually get written after the fact?"

Erica shrugged. "It's an ongoing history."

"Let's hope."

Tamis had reached the stables and dealt with the heavy door by pounding on it with his cane until someone opened it from the inside. Obviously, someone who'd opened the door for Tamis before as they danced back so the next blow missed them.

"How old is his Companion then?"

:She's not young,: Gervis answered diplomatically.

*

His room still smelled slightly musty, like no one had been in it for months. Since he hadn't been in it for months, Jors wasn't terribly surprised. Crossing, to the window, he pried it open and brushed the two dead flies on the sill outside, allowing the living fly to leave under its own power.

On the top floor of the Herald's Wing, his room had a killer view of the Companion's Field, but was so small – a little smaller, in fact, than the rooms housing the Greys – that no one had wanted it until he'd chosen it. Since he'd probably spent less than two months in it over the five years he'd had his Whites, Jors had no problem with the size. He didn't see much point in claiming space he never used.

A trio of gleaming white figures galloped across the field, kicking up their heels and playing what looked like the Companion version of tag. Even at a distance, he could see all three of them looked distinctly coltish.

:Gervis?:

:What is it?: The young stallion sounded a bit petulant.

:I was just checking to see if you were all right.:

:I'm in the Companion's Field, surrounded by Companions, on a beautiful day. Why wouldn't I be all right?:

:I just…:

:Don't like being stuck in the city,: Gervis finished his sentence. *:If it helps, don't think of it as being stuck in the city, think of it as being stuck at the Collegium.:*

:I'm not sure I see the difference.:

:Did I mention I had carrots?:

:No, you didn't.:

:And that Raya is here?:

:And you'd like me to leave you alone?:

:Yes.:

Jors grinned. Gervis and the mare enjoyed each other's company whenever they crossed paths. *:You know where I am if you need me.:*

:Companion's Field, beautiful day, Raya…:

:Yeah, yeah, I get it. You're not likely to need me.: Still grinning, he let their connection fade down to the gentle touch that was always with him and drew in a deep breath. Probably his imagination that he could taste the population of Haven on the breeze, and there was no way he could hear the noise those same people had to be making on the other side of the walls.

*

His new Whites came in time for him to attend a spring garden party at the palace.

:I can't believe this is what I'm reduced to,: he muttered mentally, delaying the inevitable by lingering at the Companion's Field for as long as possible.

:Things are quiet. Quiet is good. And you will not be the only Herald there,: Gervis reminded him. *:Perhaps you should try enjoying yourself.:*

*

"Most of the stains will come out." Lips pursed, the laundress turned his vest around in her hands. "How on earth did you manage to make such a mess?"

Jors sighed. "My Companion suggested I enjoy myself. That seemed to involve Lord Randall's eldest daughter, a full glass of wine, two rose bushes, and a desert tray."

Her brows rose nearly to her hairline. "That was you?"

"You heard about it?"

"Oh, sweet boy, everyone's heard about it." She patted his shoulder with a plump hand. "They'll be telling the story in the kitchens for years."

*

"Herald Jors?" The boy grinned up at him, seemingly oblivious to the bruise swelling his left eye shut. "The Dean wants to see you."

"Thank you…?"

"Petrin."

"What happened to your eye, Petrin?"

"Weapons training." He grinned. "I forgot to block."

Impossible not to grin back. "Now you know why you're supposed to."

"That's what the Weaponsmaster said. Me and Serrin, that's my Companion, Serrin, we can't wait to get out on the road."

Jors rubbed at the marks of thorns on the back of his right hand. "Yeah. I know how you feel."

*

"I've got escort duty available, heading south to Hartsvale, a small village up in the hills east of Crescent Lake. Interested?"

"Havens, yes!" Jors felt his cheeks heat up as Dean Carlech raised both brows at his vehemence. "Sorry. Things are just… I'm just better out on the road."

"I suspect the palace gardeners would agree with you. Herald Tamis' great-niece is to be married, and he wants to attend. Verati, his Companion, is also elderly, and we don't want them traveling that distance on their own, so your job will be to get them there and back." He looked down at the papers spread over his desk, one corner of his mouth twitching within the shadow of his beard in an obvious attempt not to laugh. "Enjoy yourself at the wedding, try not to demolish any topiary."

"It was an accident."

"Hellfire, lad!" The laugh escaped. "No one thinks you did it on purpose."

*

"So, you're the one who'll be escorting us south." Eyes narrowed, arms folded, Tamis raked a scathing gaze over Jors. "I'm not thrilled with the idea of a babysitter, just so you know. Verati and I have travelled from one end of this country to the other in our time, and we don't need a Herald barely out of his Greys assigned to keep an eye on us."

"I've been riding circuit or courier for more than five years."

"Of course you have, and I've had rashes longer. Verati and I, we'd be fine on our own, I've told Carlech that. Not that he listens, the young pup. Well, as long as you're here…" He waved a hand toward the pack on his bed. "…you might as well put those young muscles to use and carry that down to the yard for me."

"Is this it then?" Jors asked as he lifted the pack. He appreciated the older Herald's ability to travel light. He never carried more than the bare necessities himself.

"Don't be absurd… no, silly… no, *ridiculous,* boy. There's three more already down there." Fingers white around the carved head of his cane, Tamis wobbled out into the hall. "We're not riding circuit, we're going to a wedding."

*

Verati was the closest Jors had ever seen to a stout Companion.

:I wouldn't think that quite so loudly, Heartbrother.:

Jors shot a near-panicked glance at Gervis, standing saddled and waiting in the yard. *:She can't hear me, can she?:*

:Of course not, but your face gives your thoughts away.:

Tamis lifted his forehead from where it had been resting against the creamy white forehead of his Companion and shuffled aside, steadying himself on the bridle. "Herald Jors, this is my lady, Verati."

Jors bowed.

Verati inclined her head carefully so as not to topple her Herald.

:She says that was remarkably graceful considering your inclination to dive into rose bushes.:

:Why does everyone keep harping on that!:

:Because things are so quiet there's not much else happening. And speaking of harping, one of the younger Bards has composed a rondeau. It's quite good although I'm not sure 'befores' is actually a word.:

:*Befores?*:
:*To rhyme with Jors, of course.*:
:*Of course,*: Jors sighed.

*

It took forever to get out of Haven as Tamis seemed to know everyone they passed.

"Move too fast and miss the point of travel," Tamis snorted when Jors mentioned it. "Everyone has a story. And you're thinking, why should I care about everyone's story. What adventures could a cobbler… no, a butcher… no, a *whore* have that would be worth telling? That's the trouble with the young. They think there's only one story and they're the hero in it."

"I don't…"

"You'd be surprised," Tamis continued, interrupting Jors' protest. "Surprised, I tell you, if you took the time to listen. Back in my day, we listened or we got what for. I remember Shorna, one of my yearmates, she'd never ridden before she was Chosen, and one day, during a class, she went right off over her Companion's head, and Herald Dorian, she was the instructor, she said, well, at least it's a nice day. Shorna was so mad Dorian would say it was a nice day after she landed on the grass like that." He nodded so vigorously, he began to topple, and Verati had to sidestep to keep him in the saddle. "It *was* a nice day though," he added thoughtfully. "They're all dead now, you know, except for me. It's no fun getting old, boy. Although…" he gave a wet cough that Jors realized, after a moment, was meant to be a chuckle. "…it beats the alternative."

:*Speaking of old; how long can he stay mounted?*: Jors wondered as Tamis greeted a water seller with a question about her father.

:Verati won't let him fall.:

:Not what I meant. Riding, even riding a Companion, can't be easy on old joints, and I'd like to at least be out of the city before we have to stop for the day.:

In the end, Willow, the younger of their two mules, got them moving, objecting to the crowd at the Haymarket with a well-placed kick. Jors made a mental note to thank her with a carrot at the first opportunity.

*

The South Trade Road offered a wide selection of inns between Haven and Kettlesmith, and for a while, Jors was afraid they'd be staying in all of them. What had seemed like a ridiculously generous amount of travel time up in the Dean's office now made more sense.

Tamis was an early riser, but only because he napped for an hour or two after they stopped at midday and went to bed while the chickens were foraging for one last meal in the inn yards. Jors spent his evenings grooming both Companions. Verati had a disconcerting way of falling asleep the moment he put brush to withers, but then, Verati had a disconcerting way of falling asleep whenever they stopped, her head falling forward until her breath blew two tiny, identical divots out of the dusty ground.

They let Verati set the pace, and Tamis either talked about Heralds long dead…

:And Shorna was so mad Dorian would say it was a nice day after she landed on the grass like that.: Jors' silent chorus followed the inflections of the older Herald's voice exactly.

:Does he not remember he told this story?: Gervis wondered.

:I don't think so.:

:He called me Arrin this morning.:

:At least Arrin was a stallion. He called me Janis.:

…or slumped back against the high cantle and dozed in the saddle. Dozing, Jors discovered, did not cut into actual nap time.

When they reached Dog Inn and the turn east to Herald's Hill, Tamis decided to join Jors in the common room for their evening meal.

"Are you sure? Your digestion wasn't too happy after lunch."

"Stop fussing, boy. My digestion is none of your business… no, responsibility… no, *concern*."

Given how early they were eating – Tamis' digestion also had strong ideas about eating too late – even the presence of two Heralds couldn't fill the room. Four equally elderly locals played Horses and Hounds at a table on the other side of the small fire, and tucked into a corner, a merchant waited with no good grace for the smith to repair a cracked axle on his wagon.

"That's apple wood." Tamis sniffed appreciatively as he settled. "Can't beat the way it smells as it burns. Why didn't you mention *that* in your Appleby report?"

"I never noticed it."

"Of course you didn't. What are you doing?"

He'd been pulling the crusts off the thick slices of brown bread. Unless there was stew or soup to dip them into, previous meals had taught him Tamis couldn't handle crusts. Waving one of the slices, he tried to explain. "I'm uh…"

Tamis snatched it out of his hand. "Stop fussing."

"So, Heralds." The innkeeper settled at their table expectantly. "What news?"

"It's quiet," Jors told her. "The borders are peaceful, trade is good, and even the weather has been fine."

"He writes his reports the same way," Tamis sighed. "Accurate but not exactly memorable." He took a long swallow of ale, having previously announced that ale worth drinking should be dark enough to see a reflection in, coughed a bit, then smiled at the innkeeper broadly enough to show he still had most of his teeth. "You want a story, I'm afraid you're stuck with me."

:Oh no.:

:What is it, Chosen?:

:Tamis is about to tell a story. I bet you a royal it's either Shorna or Terrik up the tree.:

It was neither.

"…and although he may have defeated the first rose bush, the second, I fear, was the victor. Everyone has a story, boy," he added after a moment. "You can thank me for not mentioning your name." He likely thought the laughter would cover the comment. And it would have had Tamis' voice not been at his usual compensating-for-being-mostly-deaf volume.

On the other hand, Jors reflected philosophically, even the merchant with the cracked axle seemed to have cheered up.

*

"…and Shorna was so mad Dorian would say it was a nice day after she landed on the grass like that." Tamis gave his wet cough chuckle and tossed a stick into the fire. "I remember it like it was yesterday."

:Gervis…:

:Verati does not see that there is a problem.:

:But…:

:She says, age is not a problem. It just is.:

Jors glanced over at the elderly mare, providing a warm support behind Tamis' back and wondered if, all things considered, she was the best judge. *:What do you think?:*

He felt Gervis' mental sigh. *:I think I'm tired of hearing that story.:*

"I wanted to be a Bard, you know," Tamis said suddenly. "Good thing my lady arrived when she did or all that wanting would have broken my heart."

"Your family didn't want you to be a Bard?" Jors asked after it became obvious Tamis wasn't going to continue.

The old man started and peered across the fire at him. "What do you know about it, boy?"

"You said wanting to be a Bard would have broken your heart."

"I did? Well, it would have. Couldn't carry a tune if my life depended on it. I never forget a story though, and there's so many stories that are forgotten. You wouldn't believe the stories I found going through the old reports, stories about Heralds long dead who lived lives that should be remembered. Not because they made the great heroic gestures – those, they get put to music to inspire a bunch more damned fool heroics – but because they did what needed to be done. Those are the stories that should live on. But if you write a report that holds just the facts and has none of you in it, well, that's you gone, isn't it?" Tamis snorted. "Heralds don't die in bed, now do they?"

"Well, you're not dead yet."

Verati opened one sapphire eye and glared at Jors.

:She doesn't think you're funny.: Gervis translated helpfully.

*

At Herald's Hill, Tamis stirred three spoonfuls of honey into his breakfast tea and told a full common room the story of the merchant they'd met at Dog Inn. Later, while loading the mules, Jors saw a carter in the inn yard checking his axles.

:Oh, look, the moral of the story.:

:Chosen, that's…: The pause continued long enough that Jors turned. Gervis tossed his head, looking a little sheepish. *:Okay, it's actually pretty funny.:*

At Crescent Lake, Tamis told the story of a farmer he'd met back when he'd been riding circuit and the girl he'd spent twelve years wooing.

:He remembers every detail about that, but he can't remember my name?:

:Or that he told us about Shorna falling off her horse?:

:What does Verati talk about while we're walking?: Jors wondered, setting the pack on Willow's pad.

:How the roads were straighter and carrots were sweeter when she was young.:

:And I bet mules were better behaved,: Jors muttered, dodging a flailing hoof.

*

On their own, even with a mule, Jors figured he and Gervis could have made Crescent Lake to Hartsvale in one long day. Tamis and Verati didn't do long days.

When it started to rain about mid-afternoon, Jors pulled an oilskin cloak out of Tamis' bag, tucked it around him, and gave some serious thought to riding all night. He wanted to get Tamis out of the damp as soon as possible.

:Do you think Verati could do it?:

:I think she would try for her Herald's sake, but she is also very old. We've been travelling for some time, and she is more tired than she will admit to.:

:All right then, I'll build a lean-to.: He repeated his plans out loud as he dismounted.

"You're fussing." Tamis' protest would have held more heat had he not begun to cough.

"Gervis hates getting wet." Which had the added benefit of being the truth. His Companion had a cat's opinion of water.

"You're handy with an axe."

"My family are foresters."

"My family are foresters," Tamis repeated, rubbing a gleaming drop of mucus off the end of his nose. "What kind of a story is that?"

"A very short one," Jors grunted as he drove the first of the stakes into the ground.

*

No children ran out to greet them as they entered the north end of the village late the next day.

Gervis lifted his head. *:I smell smoke.:*

:So do I.:

Verati stopped so suddenly Willow trotted up her lead rope and smacked into a gleaming white haunch. Tamis, wrapped in every piece of dry clothing he had remaining, looking more like a pile of white laundry than a person, pulled his cane from the saddle ties. "Something's wrong."

Then a dog started barking, and between one heartbeat and the next, men and women spilled out of the houses, children watching wide-eyed from windows and doors.

"Heralds! Thank the Lady you've come, we've had…" The

heavyset woman out in front rocked to a halt and frowned. "Uncle Tamis?"

"Who were you expect…" The querulous question turned into coughing, cane tumbling to the ground as he clutched at the saddle horn with both hands.

"What happened here?" Jors snapped, pitching his voice to carry over the coughing and the babble of voices it provoked.

"Quiet!" The heavyset woman turned just far enough to see that she was obeyed then locked her attention on Jors. "Raiders," she growled. "They hit around noon, when most was out in the fields and no one much here to stand up to them. Eight or nine of them rode in and tossed a torch onto Kervin's roof. Same group as has been hitting the farms – ride in and set a fire, grab a lamb here or a chicken there, and ride out thinking no one can touch them. But Bardi – that's Merilyn and Conner's youngest girl…"

A man and a woman, neither of them young, pushed forward through the crowd and stared up at him with grieving eyes.

"….well, she's a dab shot, and she put an arrow into three of them. Knocked one out of the saddle, hit one in the meaty part of the thigh, and the third up in the shoulder. Well, they didn't like that, did they? And the one on the ground, I'm guessing he was a brother or something close to him they called their leader, because when they saw he was down, and folk were starting to run in, they grabbed her." Thick fingers closed around a handful of air. "Grabbed her and rode off."

So much for peaceful and quiet. Jors cursed himself for thinking it ever had to end. "The raider Bardi shot, do the others think he's dead?"

"No, he was thrashing and yelling."

"So they've probably taken her to trade. Her for him."

"Then why not do it? Then and there?"

"You said she injured two of them? It's hard to drive a bargain when you're in danger of bleeding to death. They've ridden just far enough to tend their wounds and they'll be back." He glanced west, at the sun sitting fat and orange just above the horizon. "Tomorrow."

"So we wait?" A voice from the back of the crowd.

"No!" Tamis answered before Jors could.

"No," Jors agreed, cutting him off. There was no need for more detail than that. And everyone knew it. Twisting around, he untied the lead line and began tossing unnecessary gear to the ground. "Which way?"

"East. We tried to follow, but they're on hill ponies, tough and fast, and we lost the trail in the rock. Nearly lost two of our own as well." Her voice grew defensive. No one wanted the Herald to think they'd given up too soon. "The hills are treacherous if you don't know them, and they do."

"We can handle the hills." He checked that his quiver was full. "I'll find them."

"We'll find them," Tamis protested, struggling to free himself from his wrappings, Verati shifting her weight to keep him from falling. "When I was a boy, I all but lived in those hills. I know their stories!"

:Chosen…:

:I know.:

But fate intervened before Jors had to speak as another coughing fit nearly pitched the old Herald out of the saddle. Would have pitched him out of the saddle had the heavyset woman not moved close enough to support his weight.

"Take care of him," Jors told her. He swept his gaze over

the gathered villagers, who needed hope as much as anything. "I'll mark the trail for those who follow."

Then Gervis spun on one rear hoof and headed east.

*

Easy enough, even as the daylight faded, to see where a group of mounted men left the track, following a deer trail into the trees.

:What are you going to do when we catch up?: Gervis asked, barely slowing.

:Depends on what we find.:

:If that woman is right, there's at least eight of them.:

:But two of them are wounded.: Bending low in the saddle, he tried not to think of what the others might be doing.

:Verati isn't happy.:

:We were sent with them to keep them safe. Safe does not include tracking armed raiders through hill country at night. I know her heart is willing, but…: Underbrush pulled at his boots. Gervis was larger than the horses they followed and was breaking a path a blind man could see. *:We'll bring them a story with a happy ending. That'll have to do.:*

When they emerged onto one of the long ridges of rock that ribbed through the hills, the sky was a deep sapphire blue and long dark shadows hid the trail. Jors dismounted, found a scar where a hoof had scraped lichen off rock. *:South-east:*

He nearly missed the point where they left the rock to go east again, but Gervis caught the scent of fresh blood, and a spattering not yet entirely dry showed the way.

:I smell smoke.:

:They must have lit a fire. They've made camp then, and we're close.:

The camp, when they found it, looked almost familiar. Jors checked his mental maps. Unless they'd traveled a lot farther from the village than he thought, they were still some distance from the border, but there was no mistaking the pattern of fire and picket line and the way the weapons had been set, butts to the ground, points crossed.

:They're army, or ex-army. Hardorn lancers.: Bow in hand, he moved carefully closer. *:I'm betting some bright officer came up with a way to use their troublemakers to their advantage. It's why they took the girl. Why they'll want their man back so badly. I bet their first order was not to get caught.:*

:I don't see the girl.:

:Neither do I. We have to get closer.:

He lifted a foot and set it down again as a rough voice growled, "I may miss you in this light, but I'll not miss the big white horse. You keep him calm, and you do what I say, and you might just survive this."

:Gervis?:

:Crossbow bolt up in under my jaw. Point touching skin.:

Companions were fast and moved in ways a man seeing a horse wouldn't expect. But were they faster than a finger tightening around a crossbow trigger? Jors couldn't risk that.

:How did he move in so close?:

:I don't think he moved in, I think we stopped right beside him.:

Not so much ex-army that they didn't have a man on watch.

*

"Let me kill him, Adric."

"He's a Herald, you idiot." Torso bare but for streaks of

blood and a field dressing on his shoulder, Adric scowled down at Jors, who struggled up onto his knees. With Gervis' life in the balance, he'd walked into the camp and been slammed to the ground with the butt of a lance. The point of that lance was now centred on his chest. "Kill one and they all come down on you."

"Then we tie him and leave him here," the first man grunted. "Take the horse with us, probably get a pretty penny for it."

:Chosen!:

:I'm okay.: More or less. *:You?:*

:He hasn't moved the bow away.:

They might not understand what a Companion was, but they'd dealt with Valdemar enough to know Jors wouldn't provoke the shot.

"We're not," Aldric growled, "going anywhere without Lorne."

"And that's why we have the girl."

Eyes adjusted to the fire light, Jors could see her now, sitting on the ground with her knees drawn up, gaze locked on his face. Fifteen maybe, no older, on that cusp between girl and woman. She looked frightened but determined. A boy, not much older, stood behind her, arms crossed, and a man with his breeches cut away and a bloody dressing on his thigh – the man who'd reminded the company about their hostage – reclined beside her.

"Not the only reason, mind you," he added, reaching over and lightly smacking her cheek.

Bardi jerked away from his touch, provoking a shove from the boy behind her. As near as Jors could tell, it hadn't yet progressed beyond touching and threat. They'd got there in time and had provided, if nothing else, a distraction. Now, they just had to get away.

He'd seen six of the eight men – Adric, obviously their leader, the one who spoke first, the one with the lance, two by Bardi, the one with the crossbow on Gervis. The other two had to be behind him, but the point of the lance kept him from turning to make sure.

"You know, I've heard stories about Heralds, and this one…" A boot impacted with his thigh without much force, more just making the point that Jors was there to be kicked. "…isn't much."

Seven.

"He tracked us over rock in the dark," Adric snorted. "What more do you want?"

"He got caught."

"Yeah, well, you can't sneak for shit wearing all that white. Get the rope, Herin, and tie him. We'll leave him here when we move out," Adric added as the kicking man moved toward the piles of gear, "but we'll kill the horse. Drive it off a cliff. Everyone knows who the damned things belong to, and we don't need that kind of trouble."

"If you don't need trouble…" Jors forced himself to look in control regardless of position or lances or crossbows. "…then you should pack up and go now. You don't think I came out here alone, do you?" He added as Adric's brows pulled in. "You don't think Valdemar is going to ignore Hardorn violating the border, do you?"

"I'll give him violating," the man with the thigh injury snarled, reaching for Bardi.

"Leave her be!" Adric snapped. "I want to hear this. Go on."

Jors met his gaze and held it. "We were already on our way out to deal with you. When you took the girl, you hastened the inevitable. Lorne is in custody, all you can do now is run for the border." He was giving them an out. If they thought they were cornered…

"All I see is you," Adric told him.

"I was out front, tracking. I've marked the trail for the Heralds following behind me."

He could hear men shifting position nervously, but he kept his eyes on Adric's face. He thought, for a moment, he'd done it.

Then Adric shook his head. "I think you're telling me a story."

"He isn't!" Bardi tried to stand, but the wounded raider dragged her back to the ground. "We sent for the Heralds after you burned down Tirin's cot at the sheephold!"

:Smart girl.:

:We will free her, Chosen.:

Adric stared at her for a long moment. "How many?"

"Heralds?" She rolled her eyes. "How should I know? I was with you when they arrived!"

:Brave girl.:

:We will free her.:

"Two lies," Adric growled, "do not make a story true." He turned, firelight painting orange streaks on his torso. "Herin, the rope!"

"Got it." Herin straightened, coil of rope on one shoulder, started back, and paused, head cocked toward the surrounding woods. "There's something out there!"

"Animal."

"Something big."

"Big animal," Adric scoffed. "Now get your thumb out of your ass and get that rope over…"

The sound of a large animal moving through thick brush was unmistakable.

:No one could have followed that quickly from the village.:

:Verati says Tamis says to be ready.:

:What?: That was all the protest he had time for as Verati charged out from between the trees, screaming a challenge as she galloped through the camp. Gone was the stout old lady who fell asleep being brushed, replaced by a gleaming white dervish ridden by a rider in white who whirled a sword above his head.

A man screamed on the side of the camp, going down under her hooves.

Eight.

Diving forward under the lance, Jors took the man who held it to the ground as Gervis answered Verati's challenge. A crossbow bolt slammed into packed dirt. Another scream nearly drowned out the distinctive crunch of shattering bone.

Verati charged back out of the trees, closer to the fire, sending the raider with the wounded thigh rolling away from her hooves. Bardi seemed to be dealing with the boy. Jors got his hands on the lance, drove the butt hard into the lancer's chest, and twisted just in time to block a blow from behind. Gervis reared. Herin dropped the rope and ran.

"Call them off!"

Jors looked down to see a lance point driven into his stomach, the edge sharp enough to cut through his Valathers. Pain caught up a second later as blood dribbled out of the tear.

"Call them off," Adric repeated. "Or I'll gut you."

"It's too late," Jors told him. On the other side of the fire, the boy threw himself up onto a horse and rode out into the darkness. Adric was now the last man standing. "You've lost."

"No."

"It's over."

"No!" His eyes were wild. His chest heaved. Blood seeped through the bandage on his shoulder. "Not possible! We were riding against farmers! Shepherds! Stupid villagers!" He spun on one heel, shifted his grip, drew back his arm, and hurled the lance directly at Bardi, silhouetted in front of the fire snarling, "Her fault."

Bardi. The lance in flight. Then a white blur.

The lance took Verati in the throat. Blood sprayed. She slammed to her knees, Tamis flying over her head.

Jors took Adric down, quickly, efficiently, not even thinking of what he was doing. Gervis was already there when he slid to his knees by Verati's side. The blood had already begun to puddle, it poured so fast from the wound.

:You can not save her, Heartbrother.:

Maybe not her, but Tamis…

The old man lay crumpled, reaching back weakly for his Companion. He still wore his scarf wrapped around his throat, and instead of a sword, his cane lay broken by his side. Jors had seen dying men before, and he knew he saw one now. He moved him, carefully, until he could touch Verati's face. She sighed her last breath against his fingers.

Tamis smiled. "Every story," he said, his voice barely louder than the breeze in the surrounding trees, "has to end."

He moved a finger just enough to wrap a line of silver white mane around it. "Stop fussing," he murmured. Then he closed his eyes. And never opened them again.

"My fault?"

Jors looked up to see Bardi standing on the other side of Verati's body, the firelight glinting on the tears running down her cheeks.

"My fault?" she repeated.

"No." He tried to put all the reassurance he could into his voice. "Not your fault."

"I just… I just couldn't let them ride in and ride away. I just needed to do something. I just needed…"

She needed her story to start.

One of the raiders was dead, skull caved in by Gervis' hoof, the rest they tied with their own ropes, trussed up by their own fire waiting for justice. Only the boy had gotten away. and Jors found himself hoping he made it safely to the border, that he carried the story home of how Valdemar's borders were defended – farmers, shepherds, villagers not there for the plundering.

Bardi helped him take off Verati's saddle then watched as he tucked Tamis up against her side. Gervis standing guard over both bodies. "You're wounded."

He glanced down. The dribble of blood had stopped before the edge of his tunic, but before he could declare it nothing, Bardi had unfastened his leathers and secured a pad of cloth against the puncture. Jors decided not to think too hard about where the cloth had come from. "Thank you."

"Yeah. Okay. What do we do now?" she asked, wiping her nose on her sleeve.

"We wait until help comes," Jors told her, moving to build up the fire. The villagers might not have followed him, but he knew, knew without a doubt, that they'd followed Tamis. One thing to let a young man in Herald's Whites save the day, and another thing entirely to let an old man do it. While they waited, he'd tell her a story. Practice the story he'd write in his report.

It wouldn't be a big heroic story, the kind that got put to music to inspire more heroics, although in the end, he supposed, it would be that kind of story too.

"Tamis wanted to be a Bard, but he couldn't sing. He liked his tea sweet, and his beer dark, and the smell of apple wood smoke. He had a yearmate named Shorna, who'd never ridden before she was Chosen…"

NOTHING BETTER TO DO

Jors stiffened in the saddle, head cocked. He could hear bird song. The wind humming in the upper canopy, leaves and twigs rubbing together as percussion. Small animals moving in the underbrush.

:Chosen?: Gervis turned to stare back over his shoulder with one sapphire eye.

:I thought I heard a baby crying.:

:Out here?:

It was a good question. They were more than a day's ride from Harbert on a path that would lead, by the end of the day, to a new settlement set up by three foresting families who'd been given a royal charter to harvest this section of the wood. Besides the usual responsibilities of a Herald on circuit, Jors had specific instructions to make sure they weren't exceeding their charter.

Jors had never met one of the near legendary Hawk-brothers, wouldn't actually mind meeting a Hawkbrother, and had less than no desire to meet a Hawkbrother because a forester had gotten greedy and begun cutting outside the territory they'd been granted. He'd grown up in such a settlement, his family still lived in one, and he knew exactly how tempting it could be to harvest that perfect tree just on the edge of the grant. And then the tree just beyond that.

Go far enough *just beyond* in this particular corner of Valdemar, and problems became a lot more serious than re-establishing the boundaries between feuding families.

An infuriated shriek pulled Jors from his reflections and sent a small flock of birds up through the canopy, wings drumming against the air.

:There! Did you hear it?:

:Given that I haven't gone deaf in the last ten paces, yes, Chosen, I heard it. But that didn't sound like an infant.:

:No.: Jors had to admit it didn't. *:Whatever it is, it sounds furious.:*

As Gervis picked up his pace, Jors readied his bow. He was reasonably proficient with a sword – he wouldn't be riding courier if he wasn't – but even the Weaponsmaster agreed there were few currently in Whites who could match his skills as an archer. It came from wanting to eat while growing up, as foresters depended on the wood for most of their meat. Small game, large; by the time Gervis had appeared outside the palisade with twigs tangled in his mane and an extraordinarily annoyed expression on his face, Jors had learned to place his arrows where they'd do the most good.

But there were predators in the woods as well, and it wasn't unusual for the hunters to find themselves hunted by something just as interested in a meal.

:I smell smoke.:

Jors flattened against the pommel as Gervis took them off the main track onto what might have been a path, might have been a dry water channel. Either way, branches hadn't been cleared for a man on horseback.

He could smell the smoke now, too, but it wasn't the heart-stopping scent of leaves and twigs and deadfall going up, it was more pungent. Slower. Familiar…

"Charcoal burner!" he said just as they emerged into a clearing.

There was the expected cone of logs over the firepit. There the expected small… well, in all honestly, hut was probably the kindest description. A little unexpected to see three scruffy chickens in a twig corral by the hut, but eggs were always welcome. Completely unexpected to see the half-naked toddler straining to reach the firepit, held back by a leather harness around his plump little body and a rope tied to a cedar stake.

The toddler turned to face the Herald and his Companion, tiny dark brows drew in, muddy fists rose, and he shrieked.

In rage.

:Well?: Gervis said after a long moment.

:It's a baby. I'm not… I don't.…: He sighed and swung out of the saddle.

The toddler stared at him in what could only be considered a highly suspicious manner and shrieked again.

"Hey there, little fellow." Jors kept his voice low and non-threatening, like he would when approaching a strange dog. And he'd *rather* be approaching a strange dog. Two strange dogs. A pack of strange dogs. He'd know exactly what he had to do to rescue this child from a pack of dogs, he just wasn't sure what he was supposed to do with a child alone.

:I doubt he's going to bite.:

Jors realized the fingers on his outstretched hand were curled safely in. "But you don't know that for sure," he muttered as he uncurled them. "It's okay, little guy. We're not going to hurt you. We're here to help."

Blue eyes widened as the toddler stared past him. Leaning against the support of the harness, he scrambled around about twenty degrees of the circle the rope allowed him until he was facing Jors, hands reaching out and grabbing at the air. "Ossy!"

"Ossy?" Glancing back, Jors thought Gervis looked as confused as he felt. "Ossy… Horsey! He thinks you're a horse." The shrieking picked up a distinctly proprietary sound, interspersed with something that could have been *me* or could have been random *eee* noises, Jors wasn't sure. *:Come a little closer, and see if he'll quiet down.:*

The noises changed to happy chortling as Gervis moved slowly and carefully close enough for the toddler to throw himself around one of the Companion's front legs. It wasn't exactly quiet, but it was definitely *quieter*.

:He's sticky.:

:Is that normal?: Jors wondered, heading for the hut.

:How should I know?: The young stallion sounded slightly put out. And then a little panicked. *:Chosen? Where are you going?:*

:To look for his parents. They can't be far.: If they were, Jors intended to have a few official words with the sort of people who'd wander off leaving their child tethered to a stake in the deep woods. Might as well tether out a sacrificial goat.

And speaking of goats, as he came up to the hut, he could see a bored-looking nanny staring at him from the back of the chicken corral, jaws moving thoughtfully around a mouthful of greenery. The fodder in the pen, still green and unwilted, suggested the parents were…

He froze, one hand on the stretched hide that covered the opening to the hut.

:Chosen?:

:I heard.:

Moaning.

He found the charcoal burner no more than ten feet out from the clearing, pinned to the ground by the jagged end of a branch through his chest. Jors could do a field dressing as well as any Herald, maybe better than a few as he spent so much time out on the road, but not even a full Healer who'd been present when the accident happened could have changed the outcome. With the branch in the wound, the charcoal burner died slowly. Pulled free, he'd bleed out instantly.

Looking up, Jors could see the new scar where the deadfall had finally separated from the tree. The charcoal burner had probably passed under it a hundred times, forgot it was up there if he'd even noticed it at all. It wasn't easy to see a branch hung up in the high canopy – Jors had lost an uncle to a similar accident when he was eight. Could remember the tears on his father's face as he carried his brother's body back in through the palisade.

The charcoal burner was older than Jors expected, mid-thirties maybe, allowing for the rough edges of a hard life – although it couldn't have helped that he'd been slowly dying since the branch had pinned him. When Jors knelt by his side, he opened startlingly blue eyes.

The knowledge of his imminent death was evident in the gaze he locked onto Jors' face as he fought to drag air into ruined lungs. "Torbin?" he wheezed. "My son?"

"He's fine."

"Take… to sister. Rab…bit Hole." A callused hand batted weakly at Jors' knee, leaving smears of red-brown against the white. "Prom…ise."

"My word as a Herald. I will put your son in your sister's arms."

He held Jors' gaze for a long moment then closed his eyes and sighed.

He didn't breathe in again.

*

The only evidence of a woman inside the hut was a faded ribbon curled up on a rough shelf. Jors set it on the pile of the charcoal burner's possessions, wrapped them in the more worn of the two blankets on the pallet, and tied the bundle off. Without a mule – and mules were more trouble than they were worth in the deep wood – he couldn't carry much more than his own gear, but Torbin's inheritance from his dead father and his missing mother was so tiny the Herald didn't feel right leaving any of it behind.

While Jors buried his father – the soft, deep loam making an unpleasant job significantly easier than it might have been – Torbin had fallen asleep curled up against Gervis' side, still secured by the rope for safety's sake. Herald and Companion both had agreed he was too young to get any sort of closure from seeing the body. Although, given that their combined experience with small children could be inscribed on a bridle bell with plenty of room leftover for the lyrics to *Sun and Shadow*, Jors could only hope they'd made the right decision.

As Jors stepped out of the hut, Torbin's head popped up from under the other blanket. He blinked sleepily, and screamed.

:He's hungry.:

:How can you tell?:

:He sounds hungry.:

He sounded furious as far as Jors could tell. *:What do I feed him?:*

:The goat needs milking.:

He looked from the goat, who continued to chew on the last few bits of fodder, to his Companion. *:How do you know?:*

:She's leaking.:

Jors had never milked a goat, but he'd been around and he'd seen goats milked and how hard could it be? After all, goats producing milk wanted to be milked.

Although he couldn't prove that by this particular goat.

As Torbin's screams grew in both volume and duration, Jors finally managed to tie the goat to a hook on the side of the hut and get the small pail he'd found more or less in position under the leaking udder, but it wasn't until Gervis moved close enough to catch the nanny's gaze and hold it that he actually managed to get his hand around a teat.

:I'm beginning to think the Collegium needs to add a few more practical courses,: the Companion said thoughtfully as Jors decanted the frothy milk into a mug with a carved wooden spout.

:I'd have been willing to lose an hour of instruction in court etiquette,: Jors admitted, handing the mug to Torbin. He'd found the mug in the hut and had to unpack it from the blanket bundle.

The child clutched it with both hands, sat down on his bare bottom, and began to drink.

With Torbin occupied, and blessedly quiet, Jors dealt with the fire pit and released the livestock.

:Will they be safe?:

:I'd put that chicken up against a Change-lion.: Sucking at a bleeding, triangular wound pecked into his left thumb, Jors dug a travel biscuit from his saddle bags and handed it to Torbin just as the child put down the now empty mug and opened his mouth to scream. *:I think I'm getting the hang of this.:*

:We need to bring the goat with us.:

:We what?:

:We were a day from the settlement when we rose this morning and it is now past midday. The child will need to be fed again before you can give him over to his aunt.:

:I was figuring I'd tuck him up in front of me and we'd concentrate on speed rather than…:

:Safety?:

Torbin's possessions having been secured with his behind the high cantle, Jors took a moment to beat his head gently against the saddle. Gervis was right. Alone, he might risk a gallop in poor lighting along a rough track bracketed with branches ready to slam the unwary to the ground, but he couldn't risk it while holding a child. If it were later in the day, he'd suggest they stay the night, but it was high summer and he hated the thought of wasting the five, maybe six hours of daylight remaining. *:If we move as quickly as possible and make no stops we should get there before full dark. I really don't want to camp while responsible for this child.:*

:Agreed. Chosen? The child is leaking.:

Still gnawing happily on the travel biscuit, Torbin now sat in a spreading puddle.

There had been two square pieces of cotton spread out on bushes behind the hut. Jors hadn't realized what they were for until it became obvious that, as practical as it was to allow Torbin to run half naked around the clearing – or more specifically around the part of the clearing his lead line gave him access to – it was significantly less practical to have him up on the saddle in that condition. Releasing him from his harness, Jors carried the child over to the half-full water barrel and scooped some of the sun-warmed water over his muddy bottom.

Torbin stared at him for a moment in shock, let loose a sound that would have shattered glass, had there been any glass in the immediate neighbourhood, and made a run for it. Given the length of his legs, he was surprisingly fast.

Once caught, he objected, loudly, to having his bottom covered.

"This is ridiculous," Jors muttered, holding the struggling child down with one hand and securing the folded cloth with the other. "I mean, it's not that I have an inflated idea of my own importance, but there has got to be someone better qualified to do this than me."

:You are the only one here.:

Torbin screamed "Ossy!" again, and with both arms up and reaching for the Companion, he actually laid still long enough for Jors to tie off the last piece of rope.

:Chosen, that looks…:

"Yeah, I know. There must be a trick to it." But as unusual as it looked it seemed to be holding, so Jors lifted Torbin up into his arms then tried not to drop him as one flailing foot caught him squarely in a delicate place.

Getting into the saddle while holding a squirming child away from further contact with that delicate, and bruised, place ranked right up there as one of the more difficult things Jors had ever accomplished.

Tucked securely between the Herald and the saddle horn, legs sticking straight out, Torbin bounced once and twisted around to look back behind them as Gervis moved out of the clearing.

Jors barely managed to catch him as he tried to fling himself from the saddle.

"Pa-Ah!"

Your papa is dead, but his last thought was of you, and I promised him I'd take you safely to your aunt, was a bit complex for a child of Torbin's age. *:What do I say to him?:* Jors demanded, holding the struggling child close, his ears ringing.

:He does not want to leave his father.:

:Yeah, I got that.:

:You can not explain, you can only comfort.:

One hand rubbing small circles on Torbin's back, the other hanging on for dear life, Jors murmured a steady stream of nonsense into the soft cap of tangled curls until Torbin reared back and, still screaming, slammed his forehead against Jors' mouth.

:I don't think this is working,: Jors admitted. He leaned out and spit a mouthful of blood down onto the trail.

:Try a lullaby.:

:He'll never hear me.:

:Not with his ears; he'll hear you with his heart.:

After twenty-one repetitions of the only lullaby Jors knew, Torbin finally cried himself to sleep, his eyelashes tiny damp triangles against his flushed cheeks.

Jors sent up a silent prayer to whatever gods might be

listening that the exhausted child remain asleep until they reached the settlement, and as he stayed asleep while Gervis' steady pace ate up the distance, Jors half thought his prayers might actually have been answered.

"What is that smell?" Head up, Jors turned his nose into the breeze which, weirdly, seemed to lessen the impact. "Okay, that's strange."

Torbin squirmed and giggled, nearly pitching forward as he reached out to grab a double handful of Gervis' mane. The odour got distinctly stronger.

The Companion stopped walking. *:I think,:* he began but Jors cut him off.

"Yeah, I know." The smear of yellow-brown on the thigh of his Whites was a definitive clue. "I bet that's going to stain."

It was amazing how much poop one small body had managed to produce. Jors distracted Torbin through the extensive clean up — involving most of their water, half a dozen handfuls of leaves, saddle soap, and his only other shirt — by feeding him slices of dried apple every time he opened his mouth. He buried the soiled cloth by the side of the trail.

:You know, if we carried this with us, we could probably use it to keep predators away from the camp at night.:

Gervis snorted. *:It would keep predators away from this whole part of the country, but I'm not carrying it.:*

Smiling, in spite of everything, at the tone of his Companion's mental voice, Jors patted down the final shovel of dirt and turned to see…

"Where's Torbin?" He'd left the child tucked in between Gervis' front feet, chewing on a biscuit.

:He's right…: Gervis turned in place, his hooves stirring up little puffs of dirt. *:He was right here!:*

:You were supposed to be watching him!:

:I was watching him!:

Jors swore and dove for his sword as a patch of dog willow by the side of the trail shook and cracked and Torbin shrieked. Gervis used his weight to force the thin branches apart then Jors charged past him and nearly skewered the goat who had followed them from the clearing and was currently being fed the remains of a slobbery biscuit by a shrieking toddler.

Apparently, sometimes the shrieking was happy shrieking.

It became distinctly less happy when Jors attempted to remove Torbin's arms from around the goat's neck. Only Gervis' intervention kept him from being bitten – by the goat, although Torbin had teeth he wasn't afraid to use.

:Are you hurting him?:

:No, I'm not hurting him.: He managed to pry one handful of goat hair out of the grubby fingers, but it was almost impossible to hold that hand and pry open the other.

"Ossy!"

"That's right, Torbin. Horsey."

:Is it wise to lie to the child, Chosen?:

:It's not a lie, it's a simplification.: "Torbin, do you want to ride on the horsey?"

"Ide ossy!"

"Then you have to let go of the goat." The goat aimed a cloven hoof at Jors' ankle as he bounced the toddler and made clucking noises that didn't sound remotely like a Companion's hooves against hard-packed dirt, but the combination was enough to convince Torbin.

"Ossy!" Releasing the goat, he squirmed out of Jors' grip and wrapped himself around Gervis' front leg.

:He's still sticky.:

Practice made getting up into the saddle this second time a little easier.

:Fast as you can, Heartbrother. We're down to half a canteen of water, one cloth, and…: "Ow!" *:Why does he keep hitting me there?:*

:Perhaps he wants to make certain you never have children of your own,: Gervis sighed as he lengthened his stride.

They reached the settlement as dusk deepened into dark. Like all family compounds in the deep woods, it was surrounded by a strong palisade designed to protect against both wild animals and bandits who might consider that isolation meant easy pickings. The gate was already closed, but Jors wasn't too concerned.

He was not only a Herald, he was a Herald holding a small child.

Followed by a goat.

Steadying Torbin with one hand, he rose in the stirrups and hailed the settlement. He caught a quick glimpse of a blond head over the wall by the gate then his entire attention was taken up by the sudden need to stop Torbin from crawling up Gervis' neck to chew on his ears. At least, he assumed that was the intended destination as "Ears!" seemed to be one of the words shrieked during the struggle.

By the time he managed to pay a little more attention to his surroundings, Gervis had entered through the palisade, the gate was swinging shut behind them, and a middle-aged woman was plucking Torbin from the saddle saying, "Oh, the poor wee mite! No wonder he's unhappy, he's wet."

"Usually," Jors muttered, dismounting.

Beside the dried blood left on his knee by Torbin's father, he had yellow-brown smears on one thigh, various fluids drying on his shoulder, vomited apple on one boot, and his lap was distinctly damp and unpleasant-smelling.

He felt weirdly smug when Torbin, still shrieking and now clearly furious, tried to launch himself out of the woman's arms and back to his. He felt understandably relieved when the woman competently prevented the launch and said, "I'll just get him straightened out and quiet, and you can explain what's happening when you're all clean and fed."

There was, apparently, a trick to making oneself heard over a screaming child.

"I assume," she continued, "that there's no emergency requiring more immediate attention?"

When Jors assured her that there was not – a combination of sign language and facial expressions supporting the answer drowned out by screams – she left him to the care of her brothers, who just as competently showed him where he could tend to Gervis, wash, and change into his other, distinctly cleaner uniform. He had to borrow a shirt.

The deep woods settlements didn't have Waystations, as sleeping outside the palisades ranged from being a bad to a suicidal idea, depending on how long the settlement had been place. Heralds bunked down with their Companions – either in the communal barn if the weather was bad or outside it if not. Some of the older settlements built a Herald's Corner that offered a little privacy, but this one, young enough that some of the logs in the palisade leaked sap, was still concentrating on getting a secure roof over everyone's head before the cold weather came.

With Gervis unsaddled, brushed down, and settled with water, food, and three little girls who stared at him in adoration, Jors headed off to the male side of the communal showers, dumped a hide bag of sun-warmed water over his head, scrubbed himself down with a bar of soap and a soft brush, and felt a lot better. His ears had almost stopped ringing.

*

"Ah, Dylan, he got broke a bit when he lost Tiria." Allin, the older of the brothers, leaned back against the wall and scratched at the edge of his beard. "Was a fine fellow before, 's why we agreed to let him set up on the edge of our grant. Got to say, I'm not surprised he ended like you found him though, Herald, all alone out there like he was, heartbroken, no one to watch his back."

"Loved his boy, though," Helena added, glancing over to the pallet where Torbin lay asleep with a child close to his own age and a large orange cat. "I expect he'd have come back to people when the boy got a bit older. It's one thing to mourn while rocking a baby, it's another thing entirely when that baby's running you ragged."

"Then he should've been heading for people a couple of months ago," Jors sighed.

"I'm sure you did your best, Herald." Helena smiled as she refilled his mug. "But what do you know about babies, a young man like you? And your Companion's a stallion too, isn't he? Never mind, my grandson's near enough to Torbin's age as to make no difference, and we'd be happy to take him in."

All his instincts said these were good people, and Jors knew Torbin would be happy here. He could get on with doing what he'd been trained to do.

Except…

"I promised his father that I'd take Torbin to his aunt in Rabbit Hole."

"Dylan wanted him sent to Mirril, did he? Makes sense, she was as near broke up when Tiria passed as he was. Girls grew up together."

It occurred to Jors as he finished his bowl of stew that it was a good thing these foresters knew Torbin's aunt. Had they not, he could have spent days trying to find her, wandering around Rabbit Hole looking for a woman related to a dead charcoal burner with very blue eyes. Well, maybe not days, Rabbit Hole wasn't that big, but it was still going to be a lot easier going in with a name. Facing another two days on the trail with Torbin, Jors was looking for all the easier he could get.

*

"There's a spring where you'll be stopping, so chill any milk you have left in it overnight and it should be good until he drinks it all. There's six hardboiled eggs in the pack; as long as the shells don't crack they'll be fine for two days, but it probably wouldn't hurt to chill them in the spring as well. Let's see, what else…" Helena frowned, bouncing Torbin on one hip. "Oh yes. I've put six cloths in the pack, but let him spend as much time without anything on his bottom as possible. It's just baby poop," she snickered, as Jors failed to prevent a reaction. "After he goes, take the cloth off him and pay attention. If he starts to pee, dismount."

"Or point him out over the trail," Allin added.

That got a laugh from most of the gathered adults and a delighted shriek from Torbin, although he couldn't have understood he was the subject of the discussion.

After checking the girth one last time – any further checking of his tack would start to look like a deliberate delay –

Jors swung up into the saddle. "I'll return when I've placed him safely with his aunt."

"There's no hurry, Herald. Do what you have to."

:Ready?:

Gervis shook his head. He'd had his mane braided by small fingers the night before, and the early morning sunlight painted ripples into some of the strands. *:As ready as I am capable of being.:*

"Ossy!"

"All right." Deep breath. "Hand him up."

*

Jors spread the sixth cloth out over the bushes and hoped at least one of them would be dry by morning. He'd done his best, but there was a limit to how much he could get out with spring water and a stick.

"Point him over the trail," he muttered, heading back to the camp. He'd moved downhill to do Torbin's laundry in the hope of avoiding contamination. It might be, as Helena had said, just baby poop, but as far as he was concerned, there was no just about it. *:How is it possible for him to expel more than he's taken in?:*

:Are you counting vomiting?:

During one of their stops, Torbin had eaten a handful of leaves he'd ripped from a bush by the trail. And some dirt. And a bug. A little further down the trail, he'd brought them all back up again. Jors had been happy – for certain specific definitions of the word happy – that he'd changed back into his stained uniform. Gervis had insisted they stop immediately and clean his mane.

:Chosen!:

He'd have never heard an actual verbal call over the shrieking.

Arriving at the campsite at a dead run, Jors found Torbin straining against Gervis' hold on the back of his smock, the Companion's teeth gripping a fold of the fabric as the child fought to get to the spring.

:He ate another bug.:

"Ossy!"

Jors scratched at a welt across his bare chest and sighed. *:At least he's not a fussy eater.:*

*

Wrapped up in the fluffier of the two blankets Jors had taken from the charcoal burner's hut, thumb tucked deep in his mouth, eyelashes a dark smudge against the upper curve of chubby cheeks, Torbin looked as though he would never consider trying to throw himself off a Companion's back causing that Companion's Herald to temporarily stop breathing. As though he'd never try to poke his own eye out with a stick. As though he'd never drop a half dead cricket into someone else's supper.

Jors settled another log on the fire and leaned back against Gervis' shoulder to watch Torbin sleep. "Why are we doing this again?" he asked quietly. He and Gervis spent so much time alone, he needed the practice in speaking aloud.

:You gave your word to his father.:

"I know but…" He dug another bit of mashed egg out of his ear. "This isn't exactly what Heralds do, is it?"

:Yes.:

"Yes?" Jors repeated, wondering if he'd heard correctly. Given the egg, he might not have.

:Yes, it is exactly what Heralds do.:

"How do you figure?" he asked, stroking one hand along the Companion's silky side.

:The Heralds not only protect Valdemar as it is but, by their actions, Valdemar as it will be. This child is the future of Valdemar. It doesn't matter if he is Chosen or he becomes a charcoal burner like his father; here and now, he is not only himself, he is the potential for everything he could be. Without him, there will be no future in Valdemar, so yes, you are doing exactly what it is Heralds do. There is nothing more important you could be doing.:

"That helps."

:I thought it might.:

"You have to admit, though, he certainly puts something like a diplomatic mission to Karse into perspective."

:It is unlikely that you and I would be sent to Karse.:

"We're not diplomatic enough?"

:Not even close. Still, a mission to Karse would involve less vomiting.:

"There is that."

*

Rabbit Hole wasn't exactly a bustling metropolis, and the second person Jors asked was able to direct him to Mirril. The charcoal burner's younger sister had married the son of a wheelwright, and they lived in the family complex surrounding the work yard. She had her brother's bright blue eyes.

Torbin tried to stick a finger into one of them, but he didn't shriek when she cuddled him, her tears falling to gleam against his curls. Maybe, Jors thought, maybe he knew this was home.

"At least Dylan didn't die alone, there's that. He had a

Herald with him." Mirril blinked away tears and managed a watery smile. "He used to tell me stories about Heralds when we were growing up." She frowned suddenly at the long white hairs Torbin clutched in one hand. "Oh no…"

:Tell her he may keep them, Chosen.:

When Jors passed on Gervis' remark, she blushed and tucked the hair into her apron pocket. "I could braid them into a bracelet for him. He won't eat them, then."

"I wouldn't count on it," Jors told her. "He likes to eat. He likes travel biscuits and egg and goat's milk. Oh, and Helena at the settlement said that the next time they bring a load of lumber out, she'll pay you for Torbin's goat. She followed us to the settlement." Torbin reached out a hand and Jors pretended to grab it and eat the fingers, making him shriek with laughter. "He likes to run, and he seems to have no idea of self-preservation, but he's a tough little guy and a big believer in picking himself up and getting on with things when he falls. He doesn't talk a lot. I don't know if that's usual for his age, but he says *no* and *ride horsey*." And *Papa,* but Jors didn't add that out loud. "He's pretty good at making his wants known."

"Ossy!"

She was smiling now and shaking her head.

"We need to get back on the trail, so… uh…" It was harder to say goodbye than he'd expected. He planted a kiss on the dimpled knuckles and released Torbin's hand. "Be a good boy for your auntie."

"Ossy!"

Mirril moved him to her other hip. "Thank you for everything you've done."

Jors thought of Torbin's father. "I wish I could have done

more." He turned, then turned again. "Do you think, I mean, would you mind if I stopped by to visit him if I'm in the area? I wouldn't be checking up or anything, I just…"

…had stains all over his uniform and the smell might never leave his saddle bags and it was entirely possible he still had egg in his ear.

"Would I mind if a Herald came by to visit my brother's son? Why would I ever mind that? Why would anyone. But why would you?" Mirril's cheeks were flushed, and she ducked her head in embarrassment. "I mean, you have so much more important things to do."

"Ossy!"

With an ease that came from three days of intensive training, Jors caught the future of Valdemar as he threw himself out of his auntie's arms.

"Actually," he said, letting Torbin slide to the ground and wrap himself around one of the Companion's legs, "I don't. Not really."

:He's still sticky,: Gervis sighed.

THE TIME WE HAVE

:*Smoke!:* Gervis lifted his head, ears pricked forward. :*Thatch!:*

They were nearly at the most eastern of the cattle-holdings that fanned out a day's travel from the market town of Devin. No one purposely burned thatch so early in the spring with no straw available to replace it.

"Go!" Jors bent low in the saddle, eyes narrowed to protect them from flying ends of mane, as Gervis lengthened his stride.

They crested the ridge, saw the cattle-holding laid out beneath them, saw smoke rising from one of the barns, saw three riders race away to the north-west.

Even with the lead they had, Gervis could have caught them – no horse outran a Companion – but then the first flash of flame showed on the edge of the barn and a horse screamed.

:Chosen?: Gervis had turned toward the barn, but Jors had twisted body and reins toward the riders.

The rider closest to them twisted in the saddle – a woman with a long, dark braid, and matching dark eyes, and a smile that faltered when she saw Jors watching. He shouldn't have been able to see her expression at this distance, but she looked surprised. She raised a hand covered in a black, high-cuffed glove, and almost without him willing it, Jors raised a hand in answer.

Another horse screamed. Then a child.

:Chosen!:

He wanted to follow her. Follow them. To bring them in. Teeth clenched, he shifted his weight to match Gervis' movements, fought to shift his attention to what was clearly the area of greater need.

Succeeded enough that he yelled, "We'll get the horses!" as they crossed the compound, pounded past a young man down with a bleeding forehead, a shrieking child barely being held back, and in through the big double doors in the end of the barn.

Terrified horses kicked at their stalls as Jors swung down out of the saddle. Ducking low under the smoke, sucking shallow breaths in through his teeth, eyes and nose streaming, he started unbolting the doors.

Reassured by the presence of the Companion, the horses charged out of the stalls into the center aisle, Gervis chivying them around toward the exit, nipping and shoving until they moved in the right direction.

"Is that it?" Jors yelled, fighting for breath as the heavy shoulder of a panicked horse slammed him into the rear wall.

:That is all the horses, Chosen, but….:

Jors' boots kicked into something soft. Yielding.

"Think I found it!" He dropped to his knees, groped along a well muscled body, felt the chest rise and fall. "Found *him*. Gervis! He's too big to lift!"

The Companion was suddenly a warm weight at his side, legs folded to bring the saddle as close as possible to the floor. *:Hurry!:*

Half dragging, half rolling, Jors got the young man to Gervis' side and heaved the unconscious body up and over. Somehow, he held him in place as Gervis rose to his feet, then clutched at the stirrup as they raced the fire out of the barn.

The compound seethed with horses and people. Two bucket brigades threw water at the fire but only seemed to add to the smoke. The child still screamed. Jors could barely make out her words over the sound of his own coughing.

"Kitties! Kitties!"

"Where?" he asked, staggering toward her.

The girl holding the child's arms looked up, lashes clumped into triangle points around blue eyes still swimming with tears. "First stall," she hiccuped. "To the left. Under the manger. There's three…"

Jors pulled off his scarf, dipped it in a passing bucket, wrapped it around his mouth and ran back inside.

:Chosen!:

:Don't worry. I'm not going far.:

The stall wasn't hard to find, but he had to search all three sides for the manger, only to find it across a back corner. He crouched, grateful for the clearer air, and groped under a board polished smooth by a rubbing horse. One. Two. He tucked the kittens inside his jacket. From the way they were squirming, he thought they were all right. The third kitten...

:Chosen! The roof is about to fall!:

Tiny claws hooked into the side of his hand. Jors closed his fingers around a ball of fluff, took a deep breath, and with his other hand against the wall so as not to lose his way in the smoke, ran for the stall door. Turned right. Figured the double doors were too big to miss and, left arm cradling the two in his jacket, right hand tucking the other up under the scarf, he raced toward safety.

It wasn't that far.

It couldn't be that far.

The fire roared in triumph as the roof collapsed.

Jors stumbled, almost fell, then hands grabbed at his clothing and yanked him clear.

He twisted in the air, hit the ground on his back, and tried, unsuccessfully, not to shriek as tiny teeth sank into his chin.

*

"I swear to you, I took more damage from the kittens than from the fire."

Gervis didn't seem convinced. Now that the horses had been confined in a corral of half-frozen mud, the other buildings in the compound were safe, and the barn was a smouldering heap of massive beams and steaming thatch, he insisted on checking for himself.

:You went back in!: Jors stumbled back a step as Gervis headbutted him in the chest. *:You're bleeding!:*

"Kitten scratches, that's all." He glanced over at the little girl on the porch with the three kittens, the mother cat in her lap.

:You went back in!:

"Heartbrother…" His back against the wall, Jors ran his hands in under the silken fall of mane and stroked the warm arc of neck. "It's okay. I came back out."

:The roof fell.:

"I know." He let his head fall to rest against Gervis' and stopped speaking out loud. *:I'm sorry I frightened you. But I couldn't not…:*

:I know. A life saved, is a life saved, and you saved three, but…:

:Don't do it again?: He felt the Companion's soft chuff of breath. They both knew that, under the same circumstances, he'd do exactly the same thing. *:Can I get dressed now? It's still a little too close to winter to run around half naked.:*

Gervis chuffed again then backed up far enough to let Jors get to his clothes. When Jors' head emerged from his shirt, he found himself still under inspection.

"What?"

:When we saw the riders, you hesitated.:

Cheeks suddenly burning, Jors busied himself with laces. "I just… I thought we had a chance to catch them."

:Three of them?:

"Yeah."

:What would we have done when we caught them?:

"They're just… I mean…" He paused. Took a deep breath. "Okay, maybe I hadn't entirely thought things out."

Gervis tossed his head. *:That was obvious, Chosen. These three are dangerous. Raya says it is very likely they are part of a gang of bandits Lord Harnin's men have been hunting for some time.:*

"Raya says?" Jors stepped out away from the building so

he could look out at the track leading to the compound. If Gervis had been speaking to another Companion, that Companion had to be close. Neither he nor Gervis had been gifted with distance when it came to mindspeaking.

:Cross country.: Gervis nudged him around. *:From the west.:*

He squinted into the setting sun and realized that what he had first thought was a patch of lingering snow was, in fact, a Herald moving quickly toward them.

:I have told Raya everything that has happened here,: Gervis said as they watched the mare close the distance. *:And she has told Herald Erica, and that will save time.:*

"For what?" Jors asked.

:For judgments, before you leave.:

Jors had planned on staying as long as any judgments required. Clearly, that was no longer an option.

"Kittens?" Erica asked as Raya danced to a stop no more than an arm's length away.

"There were three of them," Jors pointed out.

"And three riders. Gervis said they headed north-west." She twisted in the saddle, frowning up at the deep sapphire sky that preceded true darkness. "We've lost the light, and the temperature's dropping. We won't be able to track them until morning." Erica had learned some creative profanity from her two older brothers in the Guard, although she'd barely gotten started when it seemed Raya reminded her they had a gathering audience. Standing far enough away to give the Heralds a semblance of privacy. Close enough to hear.

"I take it *you* have a plan for when we catch up?" Jors asked as his yearmate swung out of the saddle. He bowed a greeting to Raya, who touched his cheek with the velvet pad of her nose.

"It's a long story."

"Supper first, then. And judgments, if the fire hasn't rendered them moot."

*

"There's fifteen or sixteen of them at least," Erica said as they settled for the night on a pile of clean straw in the milking barn's loft. Unlike the various residences, the barns were communal – thus free of any hint of favoritism – and a lot more private. Warmer too – the six milk cows kept for the family's use threw a lot of heat. "That's why I followed those three. If we could capture one and put them to the Truth Spell, we might be able to take the rest without more loss of life."

"Capture one," Jors repeated, wondering if the girl's eyes were as dark up close as they were from a distance. "And the other two?"

"Capture them as well, if possible. If not..." Erica's voice trailed grimly off.

The bandits had been wreaking havoc along the North Trade Road between Heraldston and Berrybay for almost a year. They were fast, they were smart, and they were vicious; there'd been no witnesses left behind. Lord Harnin and his people had finally gotten close enough to take arrow fire, resulting in three dead. He buried the bodies and sent to Haven for help.

"They've been holed up for the winter, and I expect your three were bored."

"My three?" Jors snorted. Down in the large box stall he shared with Raya, Gervis snorted as well, and Jors caught a faint feeling of unease from his Companion's mind. *:What's wrong?:*

:They are not your three.:

:That's what I said.:

:No, you said they are not your three.:

"They've come a fair distance from their regular stomping grounds," Erica continued, unaware of the silent conversation, "and they're just the sort to think burning down a barn is funny. I wouldn't be surprised to find they used the distraction to cut a steer from the herd and slaughter it. They'll leave most of the meat behind too, the cocky bastards."

"If it helps, they were steer-free when I saw them."

Erica reached out and patted his arm. "It helps that you saw them. The biggest problem until now is that they could be anyone. I could have sat next to one in a tavern completely unaware. I had to Truth Spell all of Lord Harnin's people to make sure none of them were involved."

"Sounds like fun."

"Yeah, well, you can do it next time. It's not like I could Truth Spell everyone who uses the road, so all we really knew was that the people actively chasing them weren't also helping them."

"That's something."

"Damned little. But now, now we know what three of them look like."

"From the back, riding away," Jors reminded her.

"More than we had," she said, yawning. "More than we had."

*

Jors still had circuit to ride, but these bandits had killed a dozen, probably more. The young man he'd pulled from the barn would have died as a result of their actions had Jors not been there. Gervis was strangely hard to convince that breaking away to help Erica track and capture one of the three was more than justified, but he finally gave in, and dawn found the four of them heading out of the compound to the north-west.

Cut deep into the mud then frozen overnight, the tracks weren't hard to follow until, in the lee of a copse of trees, they suddenly disappeared, pounded away under the hooves of a herd of cattle. Probably the same rough-coated cattle spread out along the track, enjoying the weak spring sunshine. The closest few looked up when the Heralds approached, ran a short way before rocking to a stop and setting off another bunch–the ripple of movement running through the sizable herd.

"We're never going to pick their tracks out of this," Erica muttered as Jors dismounted to get a closer look at the ground. "They could have turned, they could have headed off in any direction… we'll have to circle the entire herd and hope we spot their tracks heading out. Not to mention hope the herd doesn't spook and run exactly the way we don't want them to."

:Cows don't listen.: Gervis sounded insulted.

"Yeah, Raya says the same thing," Erica laughed when Jors repeated his Companion's observation. "Any luck?"

Crouched low, Jors pulled off his glove and ran his fingers through the impressions of cloven hooves, searching for the unbroken arc of a horse's print. Unfortunately, cows would cut a dry trail to shreds… a wet trail, with added thrown mud, they obliterated. A detail the three fleeing bandits had obviously known.

He straightened, scanned the horizon, and took an involuntary step. Then another. "This way."

"How…" Erica stopped, head cocked, clearly listening to

Raya. After a moment, she closed her eyes and sighed. When she opened them, she shifted her weight, and Raya began to move forward along the line Jors had indicated. "All right, then. Let's go."

Not long after, they found the place the bandits had spent the night.

A fox stared up at them from one end of the slaughtered steer, two crows from the other. All three wary but unwilling to leave such a prize.

"They couldn't have set the fire as a distraction," Jors noted as the Companions began to pick up speed, the trail clear again. "There's nothing to distract us from."

"Destruction for the sake of destruction," Erica snarled. "Mayhem for the sheer bloody pleasure they take in it. And the more they get away with, the more things will escalate."

"Then we make sure they don't get away with it."

"Then we'd better catch them before they get into those hills." Erica tossed her head toward the layered ridges on the horizon, still covered in snow. "Those things are crossed with canyons and gullies and some nasty ground. They get in there, we'll never find them."

*

"Do you smell…?"

"Beef." Jors scanned the sky for smoke but saw nothing rising against the low-lying grey clouds. "They're close." He pulled Gervis to a stop, pulled his bow free, and slid to the ground, dropping low as he reached the top of the rise. There, in a hollow, backs to a clump of leafless willow, the three bandits sat around a small, smokeless fire roasting hunks of meat on the points of their knives.

Jors figured they'd probably stopped here, at the edge of the plain, before heading into the canyon that he could see as a black line in the first rise of hills.

"We move along that bank of snow…" Erica's low voice washed warm against his ear. "…and they'll never see us until it's too late."

"We should ride…"

"No, they'll have loaded crossbows ready."

Now she'd mentioned it, Jors saw the butt of one bow lying close to hand.

"They've shot as many horses as people. Maybe more. Raya and Gervis can distract them, make some noise over that way, where they won't be big white targets…" She pointed past the opposite side of the hollow. "…just before we move in."

The girl threw back her head and laughed, punching the man next to her in the shoulder with the side of her fist when he reached out to pull her braid. Brother, Jors realized and tried not to wonder about the wave of relief.

"Jors? Can you do this?"

He twisted to see Erica staring at him, her expression so neutral she had to be hiding something. "What? Why…?" He twisted a little farther to see both Companions staring at him as well. *:Gervis?:*

:The girl…:

:Is as guilty as the rest.: She was. Erica had tracked them to the cattle-holding. They'd tracked them together this far. The girl was one of the bandits, and the bandits were thieves and murderers. If she hadn't thrown the torch herself, she allowed it to be thrown knowing that horses would die and not caring if people did.

:If you are sure.:

The girl threw back her head and laughed…

"Jors?"

"Of course I'm sure."

Erica glanced over at the Companions and shrugged, a quick rise and fall of her shoulders that said 'let's get on with this' as clearly as if she'd spoken aloud. It was Erica's call. She wasn't senior, but Jors had joined her hunt. Pulling her sword, she nodded toward the fire. "All right. Go."

It worked exactly as planned.

Heads started to turn as Erica rose out of her crouch, then jerked back the other way as the two Companions managed to sound like a charging cavalry unit. Jors got two shots off – confident enough in his ability to shoot past the other Herald. The first arrow pinned one male bandit to the ground through the trailing end of his jacket, the second went into the shoulder of the second male causing the throwing knife he held to slide from spasming fingers. The third…

The third…

Her eyes were as dark up close. There was grease on her chin and a perfect line of white teeth showed between slightly parted lips. She had a mole on one cheek, the flat dark kind Jors had heard girls refer to as beauty marks. Fitting. She was beautiful. Not very tall. But strong. Abandoning her gloves by the fire, she wrapped one bare hand around the horn and swung up into the saddle, deftly controlling the panicking horse. Her feet didn't touch the stirrups until she'd been in the saddle for half a dozen strides. She bent low, tucked behind the cantle, further hidden behind a sudden scud of blowing snow. He didn't have a shot.

The ring of steel on steel spun him around, and he saw Erica fighting the bandit he'd pinned. The man – visibly older than the bandit girl – had shrugged free of his jacket, but the delay had given Erica time to seize the advantage, and she clearly had no intention of giving it back. One blow, two, and he went down…

…as the bandit with the arrow in his shoulder rose up to his knees, his knife in his other hand, pulled back to slash at Erica's hamstrings.

Jors charged forward, kicked the knife clear, then pivoted and kicked the bandit in the head.

The girl was gone, the pounding of her horse's hooves growing fainter.

"She'll be nearly to those canyons by now," Erica growled.

"If you can handle these two, I'll go after her."

"Those canyons are a maze, you'll never…"

"I'm a better tracker than you are, you know I am. And she hasn't got that much of a lead."

Erica wanted to say no. He didn't know why, but he could see it on her face. Thing was, she wanted to bring these people in more, and he could see that too. Finally, she nodded.

Gervis ran past, and Jors swung up much the way the bandit girl had, bow in his free hand. As they cleared the hollow, he saw the girl reach the line of black and disappear.

By the time they reached the canyon, it was snowing hard enough Jors appreciated the cover the cliffs provided. He'd left his heavy winter leathers behind in Devin, and while the lighter clothing he had on wasn't made for extended cold weather, hopefully he wouldn't be out in it long enough for it to be a problem. *:She can't have gone far.:*

She hadn't.

Nor was she trying particularly hard to hide her trail, Jors realized as they headed up a slope steep enough he felt himself sliding in the saddle. She probably assumed her familiarity with the layout of the canyons – and only someone familiar with the ground would move so fast over such treacherous trails – would allow her to get away.

If Gervis had been a horse, it might have worked.

:There!:

:I see her!:

When she realized he was close, she put her heels to her horse. Bandit and Herald galloped single file along a narrow ledge. To the left, sheer rock rose over Jors' head. To the right, a drop of maybe twice his height down to what looked like a dried riverbed. Dangerous, but not deadly.

Except that the next time he looked, the river bed had fallen away, down a tumbled hill of rock to flatten out a considerable distance below.

The girl was brilliant rider, he'd give her that.

Jors could almost reach out and grab the blowing ends of a dark tail when her horse screamed, hooves striking wildly at the rock as it tipped to the right and fell.

She twisted around, met Jors' eyes…

Jors clutched at the saddle as Gervis threw himself back, front feet paddling at the crumbling rock until finally he stood, sides heaving, nose out over a section of the ledge that no longer existed.

:Heartbrother? Are you all right?:

Gervis didn't answer for a moment, then he said, *:That was too close.:*

:Not arguing. If you back up about fifteen feet, there's place that's wide enough I can dismount.:

He felt Gervis draw in a deep breath and let it out slowly. One foot at a time, raising it carefully and lowering it more carefully still, Gervis backed up until a cavity in the left wall gave Jors enough room to swing down to the ledge beside him and slide past.

When he got back to the break, the blowing snow and the angle of the rock kept him from seeing the river bed until he dropped to his knees.

The horse was dead.

The rider…

He couldn't see her on the river bed. If she'd been thrown…

There!

About halfway down the cliff, on triangle of a ledge about six feet long, no more than two feet wide at the narrow end. She lay on her back, one of her arms dangling, the other flung out as though she'd been grabbing at handholds as she fell.

:Is she dead?:

:I don't know.: With her head turned away from the cliff, Jors couldn't see her face.

Then her outstretched arm moved. Pale fingers flexed.

Jors crawled a little farther forward. *:I can get to her. The rock's crumbled all the way to the ledge.:* But when he went to move again, a hoof caught the edge of his trousers, holding him in place. He twisted to stare up at Gervis. *:I can't leave her there to die!:*

:Raya says Herald Erica can not leave the bandit men without shelter. Particularly not the one who is injured. She must get them to the cattle-holding before she can join us. She is…: He paused, and his ears flicked forward. *:She is not happy.:*

Jors had no idea if it was Raya or Erica who was unhappy, nor did it particularly matter. Heralds made hard choices. It was part of the job. But if Gervis could still reach Raya, they hadn't gone far.

:Gervis, you need to catch up to Erica. Have her tie the bandit

horses to your saddle, so Raya can make run for the cattle-holding while you follow at the speed of the horses. Erica needs to grab a stretcher if they have one, boards if they don't, so we can secure…: He didn't know the bandit girl's name so he gestured down the cliff instead. *:…her in such a way we can lift her out without injuring her further. Have Erica send out a rider to meet you and take the horses,:* he continued hurriedly, feeling Gervis readying a protest, *:so that you can join her as she heads back here.:*

Reluctantly, Gervis lifted his foot. *:I will go after you reach the ledge safely. If the girl is not badly injured, you and I will pull her out.:*

Jors took another look over the edge. *:That's not likely.:*

:And yet, it is possible. Tie the rope to my saddle.:

:I can't risk pulling you over with me if I fall.:

Gervis snorted. *:I know exactly how heavy you are, Chosen. I can hold you.:*

They lowered Jors' gear first, just in case. Then, gloves tucked into his belt, as little weight on the doubled rope as possible, Jors started picking his way carefully down the path of broken rock. Most of the loose stone had been swept clear when the bandit girl went over, but the route was treacherous enough that, more than once, only the rope kept him from following her horse to the river bed. The last few feet to the ledge became a barely controlled fall.

A little surprised he made it, uninjured but for a bleeding scrape on his cheek, Jors knelt beside the bandit girl.

Her heart was beating.

Legs and arms were unbroken.

Bubbles of blood stained her lips and teeth with every laboured breath.

:Broken ribs. Probably a punctured lung. We can't move her

without a board.: He jerked the rope and ducked the loops as it slithered around the saddle horn and fell. *:Go.:*

:Be careful.:

:It's okay.: Jors forced a smile he wasn't wearing onto his mental voice. *:I think I can take her.:*

:That is not…: He felt Gervis sigh. *:I will be back as quickly as I can. Herald Erica says you must stay warm.:*

Staying warm would be the trick. Between the blowing snow and the setting sun, Jors could barely see Gervis up on the ledge; a white blur moving backwards along the narrow path more quickly than looked safe.

He'd left a lot of his gear in Devin with his leathers and the mule – the cattle-holdings were barely a day apart, and he'd intended to spend a day in each and end up back in Devin – but heading out with Erica, he'd borrowed against sleeping rough. A sheepskin for insulation against frozen ground, and two felted wool blankets to keep out the cold.

But first… He looped the rope half a dozen times and carefully worked it under the bandit girl's body, tucking her one arm up to her side, securing it against her ribs, then threading the end of the rope through the loops and pulling it snug. He had to slide her onto the sheepskin or she'd freeze, but he wanted her ribs to move as little as possible while he did it.

Tenting one blanket around them – anchoring it into cracks in the rock face with arrows – almost sent him over the edge, but finally he had her safely in a triangle of felt, his pack keeping the blanket up off their faces, one corner flipped back just enough to keep the air fresh and allow a beam of weak grey light. Jors pushed the second blanket between his body and the cliff, then wrapped it around them both. The bandit girl wasn't exactly in his arms, but he couldn't have fit a horsehair between them given the width of the ledge.

"I knew you'd come for me." Her voice was weak, thready, but with their faces barely a handspan apart it was loud enough. She licked at the blood on her lips and nearly smiled. "I'm your prisoner, then."

Jors wanted to say no, knew the answer was yes, and said instead, "Are you in much pain?"

"My heart hurts. And if yours does not, then you lie in spite of your pretty clothes."

"I don't know what you mean."

Her eyes met his. "I've thought of nothing but you since I first saw you."

He shrugged as much as their position allowed. "I'm a Herald, and you are…"

"Yes." When she laughed, she choked a little, and he slid his arm behind her head to help her breathe. "I am paid for my wicked ways," she said at last. "But I wonder what you've done, Herald, that the Goddess treats you so badly."

"She sent me to save you."

"From this?"

"From this as well."

"As well?" Dark brows rose. "You're late, Herald. Years and a great deal of wickedness late."

"I'm sorry."

When she sighed, a trickle of blood ran down to mat in her hair, a dark line against the curve of her cheek. Jors caught it on his thumb. "I wasn't."

"You weren't what?"

"Sorry. Not for anything I've done. It was…" She paused long enough Jors thought she might have drifted into unconsciousness again. Then she swallowed and continued. "…an exciting life. Just after the ledge drops down to the riverbank, there's a cleft."

It took him a moment to follow the change.

"It opens into a box canyon," she continued slowly. "We have a base there. My cousins… You could take me there."

He actually considered it. Discarded it. "No. I couldn't."

"No, you couldn't. You'll choose your pretty clothes over me."

Jors wiped the blood away again. "I couldn't move you safely the rest of the way down the cliff, and I have no way to get you to the cleft, or into the canyon, or to your cousins without making your injuries worse."

She stared at him for a long moment. "Ah," she said at last. "So you don't *have* to choose your pretty clothes over me."

"It's not the clothes…"

Her free arm rose and punched him weakly in the shoulder. "Idiot. I know."

She sounded so exasperated with him that he laughed and bent his head to touch his face to her hair, breathing in her scent. "You said you *weren't* sorry," he whispered.

"What?"

"Weren't."

She made a soft chuff of sound that might have been a laugh. "You caught that? I may be a little sorry now." Her fingers closed loosely around his wrist. "Tell me about you. Tell me all the things I don't have time… to find out."

"You should rest."

"I can rest and listen. I don't want…" Her fingers tightened. "I want to be with you for as long we have."

"We'll have…"

"Herald!"

"Jors."

"Jors." She said his name like she was telling him something she'd always known. "Please. Tell me…"

So he talked. Told her about growing up in the forest. About the day he'd looked into sapphire eyes and known the forest was no longer his life. About getting his Whites. About the Demon's Den. About the charcoal burner's child. He talked, and he looked into her eyes, and he catalogued every expression, storing them safely away.

Finally, when it had gotten so dark he could barely see her, she lifted her hand to his cheek, and he paused.

"Morgaine," she said.

"What…?"

"My name, you idiot." He could hear the smile he couldn't see. "You never asked." Her fingertips were cold against his skin. "Punished…" She blinked, and it looked like it took almost all she had to open her eyes again "…for my wicked ways." When he started to speak, she moved her fingers across his mouth. "Will you… will you wait for me?"

He swallowed, nodded, and said softly, "I'll wait."

"Good." Her fingers slipped down to lie on her chest.

:Chosen?:

"A little sorry," she said, and closed her eyes.

It was very, very dark on the ledge.

:Jors? Heartbrother!:

*

Jors felt almost beside himself as he climbed up off the ledge, as he helped Erica bring Morgaine's body up, as they rode back to the cattle-holding. He told the other Herald about the box canyon, and the bandit's base, and had nothing else to say. Erica let him ride in silence. Gervis was a constant presence in his mind, and Jors kept his eyes locked on the gleam of white that was his Companion's head so he couldn't see the darkness all around.

They laid the body out in a corner of one of the barns.

"This is the beginning of the end for them," Erica said quietly. "Even if using a Truth Spell on the others gives us little else, we can take their base in the canyon, weaken them enough so we can clear them off the road. It'll save a lot of lives."

Jors pulled Morgaine's braid out from under her back, laid it gently along her arm, then pulled the blanket up over her face. When he stood, Erica closed a hand over his shoulder.

"Are you all right? When something like… like this happens…"

No one had said the word *lifebond*. No one ever would.

Jors shook his head, shook himself out from under Erica's hold, and moved blindly out of the barn until his hands touched a familiar warmth and his arms wrapped around a familiar neck.

:Chosen?:

"My heart hurts," he said.

And he wept.

FAMILY MATTERS

As there's no need to wait for a reply from Verain, you'll have time to stop by and visit your grandmother before you head back to Haven."

Jors froze, oilskin packet half in the courier pouch, and stared across the desk at Dean Carlech. Ryal Verain's holding wasn't far from the forest settlement where Jors had been raised and where most of his extended family still lived, but the dean of the Herald's Collegium did not assign Heralds the task of visiting their grandmothers. "Sir?"

"She's not likely to live forever, you know." The dean's lips twitched, the movement nearly, but not quite, hidden by his beard. "And, at her age, she'd rather not go another two years without seeing you."

"Sir?"

"She was quite insistent I do something about that in the letter. Also, your cousin…" He pulled a much folded and ragged edged piece of vellum off a pile on his desk, held it at arm's length and frowned. "…your cousin's daughter, at any rate, Annamarin, could benefit from your experience. What particular experience, she doesn't say."

"My grandmother…" Jors shook his head, trying to get the words to settle into an order that made actual sense. "My grandmother wrote you a letter?"

"Herald Jennet picked it up when she stopped by on her last circuit." The vellum flopped limply as the dean waved it, and Jors thought he saw the faded lines of old accounts on the back. "From the sound of it, *quite insistent* is a fairly good general description of your grandmother." Sitting back in his chair, the dean looked measuringly up at Jors, his dark eyes narrowed. "Is there a reason you haven't been to see your family in almost two years, Herald Jors?"

"It isn't… I mean, I don't… I've just…" Jors ran a hand back through his hair. "I've been busy?"

"Are you asking me? No? Good. Because I'm aware of how busy you've been, and while the country certainly couldn't survive without you…"

Jors could feel his cheeks flush. He hadn't meant to imply he'd been busier than any other Herald, but, in all fairness, he hadn't been hanging around the Collegium. Since he'd last been on circuit, he'd taken every courier run he could get, and, on those days he'd been stuck in Haven, he'd helped the Weaponsmaster teach the archery classes, run the Greys through a few basic tracking exercises, and had his butt handed to him consistently in the practice ring.

"…but you have a responsibility to your family as well.

Things are quiet right now, and we can find you if we need you. I think seven days should be long enough to soothe your grandmother's justifiable irritation." A raised hand cut off Jors' barely formed protest. "And I'm sure she'll inform me if you cut the visit short."

*

:But you don't like Haven,: Gervis reminded him as they made their way through the city toward the gate. Head up, neck arched, he pranced a little as a group of children called enthusiastic greetings. *:I thought you'd be happy to stay away for a while.:*

:That's not the point.: Jors forced a smile and waved at the children. *:The point is, my grandmother wrote Dean Carlech complaining about how long it had been since I'd been home.:*

:Perhaps she misses you..:

:Also not the point. My grandmother wrote the dean!:

:And because she did, we don't have to return immediately to Haven.: Gervis turned his head just far enough that he could fix Jors with one sapphire eye. *:If you had been to see your family, she wouldn't have had to write.:*

:We were busy!: It was a weak defence, and Jors knew it. *:You have no idea how embarrassing this is, do you?:*

:Nerial didn't believe her Herald was angry with you. She said he seemed amused.:

Jors gave serious thought to standing in the stirrups and beating his head against the sign they were passing under. The dean's Companion thought the dean was amused. The legendary, mystical protectors of Valdemar gossiped like a flock of crows, and given the isolating nature of the job, there was nothing Heralds like to talk about as much as other Heralds. He was never going to hear the end of this.

*

Ryal Verain's expression matched that on the small, black sheep jostling about in the pen behind him – not distrustful but definitely wary. The scent was similar as well, but Jors was careful not to let that thought show as he handed over the oilskin packet.

Pale eyes narrowed, Verain cracked the seal. "Well, that's that then," he grunted as he finished reading. The wariness had vanished, replaced with satisfaction, so Jors assumed the news was good. "I can't deny the news takes a load off, but I admit I'm surprised they sent it out with a Herald."

My grandmother wrote the Collegium.

When it became clear Jors was not going to explain, Verain nodded. "I've no reply needs sending, Herald, but if you can give us time to finish this pen, we'd be pleased to have you share a midday meal with us before you go. Where *are* you going?"

"Forest settlement, out from Greenhaven."

Verain's eyes narrowed again. "You're Trey Haden's nephew."

Jors fought the urge to remind Verain he was a Herald – his instinctive response to being his uncle's nephew, his father's son, his grandmother's grandchild – and said only, "Yes." Verain had, after all, only made a statement, not made the first move on an emotional battlefield. Lagenfield, the village closest to Verain's land, was close enough to Greenhaven that his family might have supplied wood had a closer forester not had what was needed.

"Well then, you'll have time to reach the Greenhaven Way-station after you eat and no time to get much further if you don't."

He was still speaking to a Herald, not to Trey Haden's

nephew. No one with sense rode into the forest after dark. "I'd be happy to stay and share your meal." Jors shrugged out of his jacket. "If you'll let me share in your labor."

The half-dozen men mixed in with the sheep, every one of whom had stopped working when Gervis trotted into the compound, shared a reaction Jors couldn't hear above the bleating, but given the laughter, he assumed it was at his expense. Speculative laughter, though; not dismissive.

Heavy brows rose until they disappeared under the thick grey curls. "Thank you for the offer, Herald, but we're nearly done. Just this lot to send out to join with the rest."

The rest were dotted over the hillside behind the compound like a spatter of ink against the new green, surprisingly sleek without their fleece. He had no idea that lambs actually gamboled.

"You settle your Companion, Herald Jors." The oilskin crinkled as Verain's grip tightened around it. "You've done what you do."

:You knew he was almost finished, didn't you?: Gervis asked as they headed over toward the stables.

:Hillside covered in shorn sheep, only a few left in the pen — it wasn't hard to work out.:

:So, it was an offer without meaning.: Gervis snorted.

:Nothing of the kind. I made it to acknowledge the value of his work; in turn he acknowledged the value of mine.:

:Your family values you.:

Hand up under Gervis' mane, Jors paused mid-scratch. *:We weren't talking about my family.:*

Gervis snorted again.

*

"No, they're tougher than those sheep of the Holderkin. They're hardy, ours. Can forage on their own all over these hills, even though the land's rougher than a…" Cheeks flushing, suddenly becoming aware of who he was talking to Rodney, Verain's eldest son, cleared his throat and continued without the profanity he'd been about to add. "They don't need supplemental feeding, and they may be small, but I saw a ram take down a wolf once. Well, a young wolf. They're not much for goring, not with their horns turned back so…" Grinning, he sketched the ram's horn's curl over his own ears. "…but they've heads like rock, and if they charge you, you'll know it. We don't have a lot of trouble with wolves – they tend to stay clear where there's people about – and these sheep, they're smart enough to stay out from under the trees for the most part, though they head for the highest ground about if they can. Expect to be chasing them down from the High Hills some season. You saw how they didn't have wool on their faces or legs, Herald? That's to help them move through brush," he continued before Jors could answer. "They don't get caught up so easily. And their fleece… ah, the fibres are fine and soft, not so long and coarse as those of the Holderkin. We shear them twice a year, spring and fall. Give us a few years to get this flock well established, and the finest woollens at Court will be from our sheep."

"Are they all black?" Jors wondered.

"You're thinking it's wool that won't take dye much." Rodney nodded. "True enough, but they throw grey on occasion, and I've a mind to breed to white. Still, nothing wrong with black woollens, is there, Herald." He waved a hand at Jors' Whites then back at his own dark clothing. "Black's slimming, they say."

"Husband! Did you just say Herald Jors looks fat?"

Rodney turned to look up at his wife, opened his mouth, closed it, and opened it again although no words came out. Just as Jors was about to protest for him, her lips twitched. Rodney roared with laughter, caught her around the waist and dragged her down onto his lap, where he kissed her soundly. "I said nothing of the kind, and well you know it," he declared when they parted long enough for speech. "Now, did you have something to say, or are you interrupting our talk to get me in trouble?"

Twitching her tunic back into place as she slid off his lap, she nodded across the great room to where Verain stood talking to a younger version of himself. "Ryan came in to say that ewe you're so fond of has led another revolt. If you want to keep her out of the stew pot, you'd best get over there and mount a spirited defence." When Rodney – who'd surged up onto his feet at the news – glanced down at Jors, she tugged him back to her lips by his beard and murmured, "Go. I'll entertain the Herald."

For a big man, Rodney could move quickly when he had too. He was almost across the room, already gesturing at his father and brother, by the time his wife dropped into his chair. She shook her head at the crusts left behind by his empty bowl, then turned to Jors and said, "Elane. I imagine you were introduced to a dozen people all at once, shoved into a chair, and told to eat up, so I don't expect you to remember."

He didn't. "Your husband is the younger son?"

"Middle. Ryan is older and Ricard…" Elane pointed to where a young man walked up and down by the windows, a squalling infant on one shoulder. "…Ricard is two years younger. The family runs to boys, but I've five sisters, so I'm hoping…" Her hand dropped to her belly. "…to even the odds."

There was only one thing that could mean. "Congratulations."

"What?" Her gaze dropped to her hand. "Oh. Thank you. I haven't known long; it's still so new. We haven't been married a year yet." She half turned in the chair to smile at her husband. When she turned back, she frowned. "Are you all right, Herald Jors?"

He schooled his expression before she could define it, hurriedly raising his mug. No one would ever smile across a room that way at him.

:My lips do not move in such a way, Heartbrother.:

A moment later, ignoring the smug, self-satisfied reaction from his Companion, Jors accepted the cloth Elane offered and coughed out an apology.

She waved it off. "Please, you got very little on me. And besides, we were almost relatives, you and I. My father is Dominic Heerin…"

Jors nodded in the pause. Heerin owned the mill his uncle brought their logs to.

"…and your cousin Hamin was courting my sister Tara. Came to nothing, though. I remember when we heard you'd been Chosen. It was all anyone could talk about. I'd just turned twelve, and I spent all that summer out by the track with flowers braided into my hair, hoping another Companion would come by and chose me. Eventually, my eldest sister dragged me home by the ear and told me Companions preferred useful people over those who shirked their chores."

Elane shared her husband's fondness for monologuing, Jors noted and wondered what their conversations with each other must be like. "This must have been different for you," he said. "From a house full of sisters and lumber to so many men and sheep."

"A little different, yes. But not so hard to get used to. Rodney loves this land, for all its rock and hills and the dangers of the forest so close. At first, I loved it for his sake, but I'm growing to love it for its own. And the sheep, well, you've already noticed their main failing, but he's determined to breed to white – that ewe he's defending threw grey twins this season – and he admires them for their toughness as much as the fine wool of their fleece. My sisters say, when they see me now, I've nothing to talk of but sheep and Rodney. Well, Rodney and sheep." Her laugh drew her husband's head around, and he paused in his argument long enough to toss a smile in her direction. "It's always the way though, isn't it, as you move between birth family and found family. This is what made me…" She held out one hand palm up and then the other. "…and this is what I am. And I'll tell you this much, Herald Jors…" She winked and stood as her father-in-law approached. "…shepherds have much softer hands than men who toss lumber about all day."

*

The Waystation was empty and quiet – although Jors supposed that, given the former, the latter went without saying. Hands cupped around a mug, he sat in the doorway and watched Gervis grazing, his coat gleaming silver in the twilight.

Beyond the Companion, in under the trees, it was already night. At the settlement, the gates would be closed, animals and people penned in safely, the youngest and the eldest would be preparing for bed, and everyone else would soon follow. Lamplight might extend the day in Haven, but out here sunrise and sunset still defined people's lives.

Not so different than from where he'd just come. Barring the differences between trees and sheep. And the difference between *Herald Jors* and *Jors with a Companion.*

:There is no difference between Herald Jors and Jors with a Companion. They are both you.:

"My grandmother would agree. Although she'd think they both mean Jors with a Companion."

Gervis lifted his head and turned to stare. Jors wished, not for the first time, he could pick up his Companion's thoughts as easily as Gervis picked up his. Finally, the young stallion snorted and bent back to the grass. *:If you are still annoyed with her about the letter, tomorrow you may tell her it was inappropriate.:*

"Yeah." Jors drained the mug and set it to one side. "Like that'll happen."

*

He didn't recognize the girl running down the track toward him until she skidded to a stop, bowed elaborately – one plait surrendering, spilling her dark blonde hair down over her face – looked up, and grinned. "Herald Jors. Wondrous One."

:I like her.:

Jors returned the grin and swung out of the saddle. "Annamarin."

In the time he'd been gone, she'd crossed from child to girl. She'd be eleven now, almost twelve, the same age Elane had been when she'd spent the summer with flowers in her hair waiting for a Companion. Instead of flowers, Annamarin's hair held a trio of feathers stuffed into the top of the remaining braid.

"You weren't waiting out here hoping to be Chosen, were you?" Grandmother's letter *had* said Annamarin could benefit from his experience.

"No! No offence," she added quickly to Gervis, dipping into another elaborate bow. "Companions choose as Companions will, and Companions will as Companions please."

:I really like her.: Gervis said as Jors worked that through.

"May I give you greetings, cousin?"

"May you what?"

She sighed, a simple exhalation defining her as the most put-upon creature in these woods. "Can I hug you?"

"Why couldn't you?"

"You're a Herald! In Whites! And I'm tragically soiled, though 'tis naught but good clean dirt." "'Tis naught?"

Annamarin rolled her eyes. "It means it isn't. Sort of. Wait…my pipes!" She pulled a set of reed pipes out from behind her waistband. "I don't want them to be tragically crushed! I made them myself," she continued after an emphatic hug that rocked Jors back onto his heels. "Well, Lyral – she got stuck here for almost a week during fall storms when the mud was up over her boots – she showed me how. But I made them. Mostly."

"Lyral?" As they walked toward the settlement, Jors ran through the names of the Bards he knew and came up short.

"She's a minstrel. She travels. She sings. She's the best. I wanted to go with her when she left, but Mama said no. Papa said good riddance." Annamarin blew across the top of the pipes and back. The rise and fall of the twelve notes sounded like a giggle. "He was kidding."

"What did Lyral say when you said you wanted to go with her?" It wouldn't be the first time a "minstrel" had discovered a talent in a child and made promises in order to lure that child away. If Lyral was one of those predators – however unsuccessful this time – Jors needed to find her. He'd be in and out of the settlement so quickly his grandmother would no doubt feel herself justified writing another letter to the dean. Beside him, Gervis had both ears flicked forward.

This time, the twelve notes sounded resigned. And a bit annoyed. "She said she didn't travel with children, but she'd be back this way in a year or two, and if I still wanted to go, we'd talk."

"About what?"

"About me going with her, I guess. I dunno." She shrugged a skinny shoulder then bent back to the pipes and blew out a string of birdsong that drew answers from the surrounding trees.

"Did Lyral teach you to do that?"

The look Annamarin shot him reminded him chillingly of their grandmother. "It's a calling bird song, Jors. You spend way too much time in the city. It's tragic."

"Can't argue with that." So, since she couldn't have known they'd be arriving today… "Shirking chores?"

"No." When he glanced down at her, she grinned. "Maybe a little. Sometimes…" She turned in place and walked backwards, staring down the track toward Greenhaven. "I just want to know what's out there. You know what I mean?"

He'd never given the world beyond the forest and the settlement any thought before he'd been Chosen. One morning they'd opened the gate and he'd found himself falling into sapphire eyes, hearing an emphatic *finally* in his head. Now he thought on it, Gervis had sounded a lot like Annamarin.

:I was tired of waiting for you. Most of those who are to be Chosen find their way to Haven.:

:If I'd known you were out there, I'd have met you halfway.:
"Jors?"

He smiled down at her. "Yeah, I know what you mean."

As they came out of the trees and into the clearing in front of the palisade, Jors found himself studying the area with a professional eye. The settlement's grant allowed a certain area cleared for living space, and it looked as though his uncle had recently expanded out as far as he was legally allowed. The edges still looked rough and raw, and he thought he saw two new buildings within the walls.

His mother's geese saw them first. Heads low, necks extended, the current flock charged out through the open gate, hissing, wings beating at the air. When Gervis lowered his own head and pawed the ground, they wheeled neatly to the left, circling the willow fencing around the vegetable garden as though that had been their destination all along. A familiar voice shouted from the garden, and as Jors and Annamarin drew even with the opening, their grandmother emerged, threw her cane at the geese, spotted Gervis, and rocked to a stop.

"As I live and breathe! The boy is back!" Less considerate of his Whites than Annamarin, she stumped forward and dragged him up against her generous bosom, leaving a smear of rich black earth across his tunic and down one leg. Given the amount of dirt on her hands, he didn't want to think about the places she'd gripped him.

It was the same possessively affectionate hug he'd always had from her, and it made him feel seven, ten, fourteen…

"You've filled out," she clucked as she pushed him back out to arm's length and looked him up and down. "Well, you couldn't have stayed all arms and legs forever, I suppose, could you? Never mind," she cut him off as he opened his mouth. "How long can you stay?"

"Seven days, unless I'm needed."

"Needed." Gran rolled her eyes. "I think they can manage without you for so short a time. Annamarin, get my cane would you, sweetheart. Had her head turned by a minstrel," she added as the girl cautiously approached the geese. Either his grandmother had gotten a little deaf or she didn't care if she were overheard. Jors leaned toward the latter. "Fool woman put foolish ideas into the girl's head. I want you to tell her that it's one thing to have a Companion suddenly appear and declare you special…" She nodded to Gervis, who nodded back. "…and another thing entirely to declare it yourself. Now, come on." Hand tucked in the crook of his elbow, she tugged him toward the gate. "It's bread day. Your mother can't leave the kneading."

His mother dusted him with flour and clucked at the length of his hair then spun him around in time to have his brother's wife Tora catch him up in a hug redolent with the scent of the first wild strawberries.

"Oh, stop making such a fuss over him," Gran snorted. "He's just come home; he hasn't saved the country single-handed."

Seven, ten, fourteen…

When he tried to step away, he discovered he had a toddler wrapped around each leg. They held him in place long enough for Annamarin's mother to appear, and while she was exclaiming over his appearance, Jors' cousin Tomlin, Uncle Trey's youngest…

"Took an axe to the thigh last fall, poor thing."

…limped into the summer kitchen followed by the rest of the settlement's children, four dogs, and a goat.

He only managed to free himself from their welcome by reminding them he had a Companion to tend to.

*

Jors set the saddle aside and let his forehead fall to thump against Gervis' withers.

:They're glad to see you.:

:I know. And I'm glad to see them.:

:But?:

:But I'm Jors with a Companion.:

:You are my Chosen.: Gervis' mental voice was matter-of-fact. *:Why do you need to be anyone else?:*

:I don't… That isn't…: He turned to rest his cheek against the warmth and ran a hand up under Gervis' mane. *:Am I a terrible person?:*

:No. You are a Herald. You can not be a Herald and a terrible person. Therefore you are not a terrible person.: Responding to a non-verbal prompt, Jors scratched along the arc of his neck. *:It is not terrible for you to want your family to see you as you are, not as you were.:*

"See, lo, where yonder Herald stands!"

Jors turned to see Annamarin just inside the lean-to, barely visible over an armload of hay.

"I know it's tragic," she said, "but this is the best of what's left. There's not a lot of grazing yet, but Mika's been taking the goats to the south clearing if the Wondrous One doesn't mind sharing."

"His name is Gervis. Have you forgotten?"

"He's too beautiful for a name." She spread her arms, the hay dropping into the manger. "He is a song walking above the mud we less lovely creatures tread upon."

:Have I mentioned that I like her?:

:You have.: Jors pulled his brushes from the saddlebag. "Trust me, he walks in plenty of mud."

"Can I help?"

"You could play something for me."

"I only know three real songs." But she perched on the edge of the manger and pulled out her pipes. "Mostly, I just twiddle, you know, make stuff up."

Jors draped his jacket beside her then bent to brush the dirt from Gervis' rear leg. "So, make stuff up."

He didn't know what he'd expected, but her twiddles were just that; random notes strung together. Not unpleasant, but not exactly music either.

:You know what you expected.: One hoof up on Jors' knee, Gervis rested his weight against Jors' shoulder. Jors grunted and pushed back.

"Annamarin!"

The twiddling stopped. Jors dropped the hoof and straightened. Their grandmother looked between the two of them and snorted. "That woodbox won't fill itself, child. And no one will be pleased if the bread is baked only half through. Don't look to him!"

"He's a Herald!" Annamarin declared as she jumped down.

"Am I blind now? Woodbox!"

"If this labour ruins my hands and I can tragically no longer play, you'll weep with sorrow at the loss!"

"If that woodbox doesn't get filled, you'll be sorrier. And you," Gran added as Annamarin ran off. "Did you think I wanted you to encourage such nonsense? I will smack that minstrel if she returns. Filling the child's head with clouds. You need to tell her what comes of running off, away from one's family in search of adventure."

"Gran, I…"

"You didn't run off, did you? You rode. It'd be different for that one, wouldn't it? There'd be no pretty white clothes and a sense of self-importance for her. She needs to know what's out there, doesn't she? And she needs to know what's here. Safety, security, no one goes to bed hungry – your grandfather and I created this from nothing, I'll thank you to remember. You missed a spot, there on the left leg above the hock." Shaking her head, she met Gervis' eyes. "I'm sure he does his best. He never was much for chores, either, always off in the woods with a bow. Still, I'm pleased to see you don't look like he's been neglecting you. He missed another spot there…"

*

His Uncle Trey, his father, and his older cousins came home at twilight. They'd spent the day marking trees to be cut when the ground dried; those that had been winter killed and those topped off in spring storms. Jors was astounded to see that Uncle Trey, a mountain of a man with more energy than any three combined, was now almost entirely grey and his broad shoulders had begun to stoop.

"We'll put you to work tomorrow, lad!" Cheeks flushed, his uncle clapped him one shoulder, looked a little surprised when Jors didn't so much as sway, and added, "I'm sure you've forgotten what hard work's like."

*

Breakfast the next morning was porridge and berries – the berries offered slightly squashed from his nephew's fingers. The boy shrieked with laughter as Jors pretended to eat the fingers, too. When his mother ruffled his hair as she bustled past the long table, he realized too late he was *becoming* the Jors that was. The Jors they all still believed him to be.

"You'll work with your father and I," Uncle Trey declared on the way out of the common dining hall.

Jors paused, half into a borrowed jacket. "With both of you?"

"Is that a problem?" Gran demanded.

"I imagine you've forgotten most of your forest craft," his uncle said.

The day would be a test then.

Jors didn't tell them he'd tracked harder quarry over the last few years than pheasant and deer – mostly because he couldn't figure out a way to do it that wouldn't sound like bragging. And while he'd done plenty of hard work as a Herald, he'd forgotten how hard *this* work was, so, as the day went on he kept his mouth shut.

"Let it go, Trey," his father laughed at last. "My boy's still the best tracker in the family, for all he spends most of his time with his ass in a saddle."

"Wasted skills," Uncle Trey sighed.

When they stopped at midday, they'd nearly reached the western edge of the grant. Sitting together on a rock shelf, they divided up the food they'd been carrying, and when they were settled, Jors' uncle smacked his arm with the side of his fist and nodded toward a stand of beech, four good-sized trees that had all been topped off. "What do you think, lad?"

"No point saving them," Jors noted, accepting a biscuit. "Best to take them down and open a hole for new growth. It's beech. The mill will take them for short boards if you stack them now and come back when the ground is dry enough for the sled and the oxen. And there's enough limb wood there to keep the ovens going."

"Well done," his father crowed. "Couldn't expect a better answer than that, Trey."

The other man snorted, straightened, and stared into the distance. "Pity we can't see if you've remembered how to shoot," he said. "Look at the size of that stag."

Jors stood up on the rock to give himself a better angle. Frowned. The distant silhouette was off slightly. "I don't think that's a stag. I think it's a Dyheli."

"Don't be daft. We're too far north. Puts on a pair of white trousers and suddenly everything's got to be all mystical. You need to keep your head in the real world. Off you go and track it then."

Jors raised a hand as the Dyheli disappeared into the trees and turned to see both men watching him expectantly. "No," he said.

Uncle Trey began a protest, but stopped when Jors met his gaze.

His father suddenly directed all his attention to the packs.

"Well..." His uncle sounded as uncertain as Jors had ever heard him. "...we'd best be starting back then..."

*

Hands wrapped around his empty mug, Jors watched his brother and his sister-in-law carry the sleeping twins out of the large family room in the settlement's first building, his brother more than willing to leave their conversation when Tora beckoned him home.

"Why are you sad?"

He made room for Annamarin on the bench. "I'm not sad."

"You don't look sad," she said, frowning up at him, "but under how you look, you're sad." Head cocked, she studied his face. "Is it a tragic love story?"

A dying bandit girl and the knowledge that he was hers and always would be. He started to say it was more complicated than that. Started to say their time had been too short for a story. Watched the door close behind his brother and his brother's family and said only, "Yes."

Annamarin nodded with all the wisdom of nearly twelve. "I thought so." Reaching into her pocket, she pulled out a honey candy, picked off a bit of lint, and held it out to him. "My mama makes these. When I had my heart tragically broken by Vernin at the mill, they helped."

"Thank you."

She dropped it in his hand, although it stuck for a moment to her fingers, and ran to join the children being herded off to bed.

The candy melted on his tongue, so sweet it nearly made his eyes water. If it didn't help, it didn't hurt.

Although, he realized, other parts of him did. Jors grunted as he stood, stretched out his back and tried to work the knots from his right arm. Hard to believe he'd only been walking and using a hatchet. He hadn't hurt like this since he'd first learned to ride.

"Used muscles you haven't for a while, lad!" Uncle Trey laughed. "Not so easy keeping up with an old man is it?"

"Leave him be, Trey, there's a trick to walking on uneven ground," Jors' father called out. "I expect he's lost the knack of it."

"He needs to come home more often," one of his cousins called.

"A few more days of honest labour, and he'll be his old self again," laughed another.

:Chosen, there's someone coming.:

A moment later, the geese sounded the alarm.

*

"He went out yesterday looking for that damned ewe he's so fond of. She'd slipped the dogs, late afternoon, and had headed for the hills with her lambs." One of Verain's men sagged against the hands that held him as his horse, sides wet with sweat, stumbled and nearly went to her knees just inside the gate. "When the sun went down, he didn't come in. Nearly had to tie Elane to the chair to keep her from heading out to find him. But he's smart, Rodney is, and he'd have found a safe place for the night, yeah, and then he'd be back by day we told her, back with that damned ewe."

"But he wasn't." Jors stepped aside as Annamarin's father pushed past, heading for the horse.

"No. We looked Herald, but we couldn't find him, not even a body or sign of a struggle or the damned sheep, and Elane sent me to find you, and I damned near killed the mare, but Elane..." He closed his eyes for a heartbeat, and when he opened them again they shone with reflected pain, obvious even in the light of half a dozen flickering lamps. "She's taking it terrible hard."

Jors closed his hand around the man's shoulder, felt the fine tremble of exhaustion through shirt and jacket, felt the tension relax as he squeezed. Pivoting on one heel, he headed for the Herald's Corner, not needing a lamp to find the way to where Gervis waited.

"Jors!"

Habit stopped his feet at the sound of his grandmother's voice.

"Where are you going, then?" She stood in the door they'd left open when they'd rushed outside, her hair, unplaited for the night, spilling around her shoulders.

"I'm going where I'm needed. To find Rodney."

Heads pivoted as the men and women in the courtyard turned their attention back to the old woman.

"I understand you want to help, Jors, but it's forest trail all the way. Wait till day and go then if you must. There's men already searching for young Rodney who know the ground. What can you bring to the search that they can't?"

"Hope." Bare feet sticking out from under her nightshirt, Annamarin moved to Jors' side and swept a steady gaze over her family. "When a Herald of Valdemar rides, hope rides with him. Yes, they have men who know the ground, but with one of theirs lost in the forest for going on two nights now, what they need is hope." She paused, then, just before the silence stretched to the breaking point, she spread her hands and added, "And they need the best tracker this family has ever had."

A further heartbeat's silence, then a cheer.

Jors bent and kissed the top of her head. *:Heartbrother…:*
:I am well rested. We can be there before dawn.:

*

"Oh, it's so horribly tragic that one of the lambs died!"

Jors sighed. "I tell you a story of a gallant ride through the night, beset on all sides by terrible dangers, finishing, with the sun barely up, in the kind of tracking that one person in thousands could do in order to save a man's life, and you're upset about a lamb?"

"It died." Annamarin released her grip on his sleeve to fold her arms. "And it was *tragic.*"

Rodney had been returned to Elane from the bottom of a crevasse with a broken leg, the ewe and her remaining lamb had been returned to the flock, and Jors had returned to Trey Haden's settlement.

Annamarin had met him on the track.

:It seems that you want your family to behave in ways you do not wish to behave yourself.:

:I don't know what you…:

Gervis gave a little buck. *:The girl has Talent. Speak to your grandmother on her behalf.:*

*

"A Bard?" Their grandmother swept a narrowed-eyed gaze from Jors to Annamarin and back. "Are you certain?"

"A certain as I can be, not being a Bard myself." Jors watched her expression change, her hand begin to rise, and knew she had just asked herself, *What would Jors know about Bards?* "Gervis," he added quickly, "is certain."

"Well…" She nodded slowly. "…that's different then, isn't it?" Reaching out, she took Annamarin's hand and tugged her close. "Are you sure you want to be a Bard, child?"

Annamarin rolled her eyes. "It's not something you *do*, Gran, it's something you *are.*"

The old woman snorted. "It's not something *I* am."

"Well, no," Annamarin admitted. "But it's like what Jors is."

"Please, child, he was Chosen. That has nothing to do with what he is, and everything to do with his Companion."

"With his Companion finding him worthy."

"What?"

Sighing, Annamarin tugged her hand free so she could gesture expansively. "There isn't a Jors before and a Jors after, Gran. There's just Jors. And Jors is a Herald."

:From the mouths of babes.:

"My point exactly." Gran grinned triumphantly and whacked Jors on the shins with her cane.

When Annamarin frowned, Jors shook his head.

*

"Try again when you're older," he told her later when they were walking away from the settlement, down the track toward Greenhaven.

"It's *tragic* she doesn't understand!"

"It's a little annoying," he admitted. "But, in the end, I know who I am."

:You know who you are outside the palisades.: Jors jumped as Gervis' tail slapped against the back of his legs. *:And staying away solves nothing,:* the Companion added.

:Not every problem can be solved. Or needs to be.: Out loud he said, "There'll be Bards visiting this summer."

"How do you know?"

"I'm a Herald." He grinned. "I know things. And, in a couple of years, I'll see you in Haven."

:You hate staying in Haven.:

:I didn't say I was going to stay. I just said I'd see her there.:

:And then tragically abandon her?:

:Stop it.:

"You don't look so sad when you talk to him in your head." She planted her feet and struck a dramatic pose. "This is as far as I'm allowed to go. Can I hug you? I'm clean."

"You could hug me if you were dirty," he told her.

She shook her head, one plait falling loose. "That would be so tragically wrong."

Hugging Annamarin had nothing to do with being seven or ten or fourteen. When hugged her, as her cousin and a Herald, he hugged the future, not the past.

:You didn't tell your grandmother she shouldn't write to the Dean,: Gervis pointed out when Jors was in the saddle and there was nothing but open road before them.

:I know. I was afraid it would only encourage her.:

Gervis snorted. *:You were afraid.:*

:That too. But the last thing I need is Gran and the dean starting up a correspondence.: Jors twisted and looked back toward the settlement. Annamarin must have reached the end of the track because he could just hear the geese protesting her return. *This is what made me.* He settled back in the saddle. *This is what I am.*

Birth family. Found family.

:Pick up the pace, Heartbrother, let's go home.: